MOONLIGHT
Maupassant Original Short Stories
Volume IX

Guy de Maupassant

iBoo Press
London

MOONLIGHT
Maupassant Original Short Stories

Volume IX

Guy de Maupassant

Translated by
ALBERT M. C. McMASTER, B.A.
A. E. HENDERSON, B.A.
MME. QUESADA and Others

Published by
iBoo Press House

3rd Floor
86-90 Paul Street
London, EC2A4NE UK

t: +44 20 3695 0809
info@iboo.com II iBoo.com

ISBNs
978-1-64181-747-9 (p)

Printed in the United States

MOONLIGHT
Maupassant Original Short Stories

Volume IX

Guy de Maupassant

VOLUME IX

TOINE

He was known for thirty miles round was father Toine—fat Toine, Toine-my-extra, Antoine Macheble, nicknamed Burnt-Brandy—the innkeeper of Tournevent.

It was he who had made famous this hamlet buried in a niche in the valley that led down to the sea, a poor little peasants' hamlet consisting of ten Norman cottages surrounded by ditches and trees.

The houses were hidden behind a curve which had given the place the name of Tournevent. It seemed to have sought shelter in this ravine overgrown with grass and rushes, from the keen, salt sea wind—the ocean wind that devours and burns like fire, that drys up and withers like the sharpest frost of winter, just as birds seek shelter in the furrows of the fields in time of storm.

But the whole hamlet seemed to be the property of Antoine Macheble, nicknamed Burnt-Brandy, who was called also Toine, or Toine-My-Extra-Special, the latter in consequence of a phrase current in his mouth:

"My Extra-Special is the best in France:"

His "Extra-Special" was, of course, his cognac.

For the last twenty years he had served the whole countryside with his Extra-Special and his "Burnt-Brandy," for whenever he was asked: "What shall I drink, Toine?" he invariably answered: "A burnt-brandy, my son-in-law; that warms the inside and clears the head—there's nothing better for your body."

He called everyone his son-in-law, though he had no daughter, either married or to be married.

Well known indeed was Toine Burnt-Brandy, the stoutest man in all Normandy. His little house seemed ridiculously small, far too small and too low to hold him; and when people saw him standing at his door, as he did all day long, they asked one another how he could possibly get through the door. But he went in whenever a customer appeared, for it was only right that Toine should be invited to take his thimbleful of whatever was drunk in his wine shop.

His inn bore the sign: "The Friends' Meeting-Place"—and old

Toine was, indeed, the friend of all. His customers came from Fecamp and Montvilliers, just for the fun of seeing him and hearing him talk; for fat Toine would have made a tombstone laugh. He had a way of chaffing people without offending them, or of winking to express what he didn't say, of slapping his thighs when he was merry in such a way as to make you hold your sides, laughing. And then, merely to see him drink was a curiosity. He drank everything that was offered him, his roguish eyes twinkling, both with the enjoyment of drinking and at the thought of the money he was taking in. His was a double pleasure: first, that of drinking; and second, that of piling up the cash.

You should have heard him quarrelling with his wife! It was worth paying for to see them together. They had wrangled all the thirty years they had been married; but Toine was good-humored, while his better-half grew angry. She was a tall peasant woman, who walked with long steps like a stork, and had a head resembling that of an angry screech-owl. She spent her time rearing chickens in a little poultry-yard behind the inn, and she was noted for her success in fattening them for the table.

Whenever the gentry of Fecamp gave a dinner they always had at least one of Madame Toine's chickens to be in the fashion.

But she was born ill-tempered, and she went through life in a mood of perpetual discontent. Annoyed at everyone, she seemed to be particularly annoyed at her husband. She disliked his gaiety, his reputation, his rude health, his embonpoint. She treated him as a good-for-nothing creature because he earned his money without working, and as a glutton because he ate and drank as much as ten ordinary men; and not a day went by without her declaring spitefully:

"You'd be better in the stye along with the pigs! You're so fat it makes me sick to look at you!"

And she would shout in his face:

"Wait! Wait a bit! We'll see! You'll burst one of these fine days like a sack of corn-you old bloat, you!"

Toine would laugh heartily, patting his corpulent person, and replying:

"Well, well, old hen, why don't you fatten up your chickens like that? just try!"

And, rolling his sleeves back from his enormous arm, he said:

"That would make a fine wing now, wouldn't it?"

And the customers, doubled up with laughter, would thump the table with their fists and stamp their feet on the floor.

The old woman, mad with rage, would repeat:

"Wait a bit! Wait a bit! You'll see what'll happen. He'll burst like a sack of grain!"

And off she would go, amid the jeers and laughter of the drinkers.

Toine was, in fact, an astonishing sight, he was so fat, so heavy, so red. He was one of those enormous beings with whom Death seems to be amusing himself—playing perfidious tricks and pranks, investing with an irresistibly comic air his slow work of destruction. Instead of manifesting his approach, as with others, in white hairs, in emaciation, in wrinkles, in the gradual collapse which makes the onlookers say: "Gad! how he has changed!" he took a malicious pleasure in fattening Toine, in making him monstrous and absurd, in tingeing his face with a deep crimson, in giving him the appearance of superhuman health, and the changes he inflicts on all were in the case of Toine laughable, comic, amusing, instead of being painful and distressing to witness.

"Wait a bit! Wait a bit!" said his wife. "You'll see."

At last Toine had an apoplectic fit, and was paralyzed in consequence. The giant was put to bed in the little room behind the partition of the drinking-room that he might hear what was said and talk to his friends, for his head was quite clear although his enormous body was helplessly inert. It was hoped at first that his immense legs would regain some degree of power; but this hope soon disappeared, and Toine spent his days and nights in the bed, which was only made up once a week, with the help of four neighbors who lifted the innkeeper, each holding a limb, while his mattress was turned.

He kept his spirits, nevertheless; but his gaiety was of a different kind—more timid, more humble; and he lived in a constant, childlike fear of his wife, who grumbled from morning till night:

"Look at him there—the great glutton! the good-for-nothing creature, the old boozer! Serve him right, serve him right!"

He no longer answered her. He contented himself with winking behind the old woman's back, and turning over on his other side—the only movement of which he was now capable. He called this exercise a "tack to the north" or a "tack to the south."

His great distraction nowadays was to listen to the conversations in the bar, and to shout through the wall when he recognized a friend's voice:

"Hallo, my son-in-law! Is that you, Celestin?"

And Celestin Maloisel answered:

"Yes, it's me, Toine. Are you getting about again yet, old fellow?"

"Not exactly getting about," answered Toine. "But I haven't

grown thin; my carcass is still good."

Soon he got into the way of asking his intimates into his room to keep him company, although it grieved him to see that they had to drink without him. It pained him to the quick that his customers should be drinking without him.

"That's what hurts worst of all," he would say: "that I cannot drink my Extra-Special any more. I can put up with everything else, but going without drink is the very deuce."

Then his wife's screech-owl face would appear at the window, and she would break in with the words:

"Look at him! Look at him now, the good-for-nothing wretch! I've got to feed him and wash him just as if he were a pig!"

And when the old woman had gone, a cock with red feathers would sometimes fly up to the window sill and looking into the room with his round inquisitive eye, would begin to crow loudly. Occasionally, too, a few hens would flutter as far as the foot of the bed, seeking crumbs on the floor. Toine's friends soon deserted the drinking room to come and chat every afternoon beside the invalid's bed. Helpless though he was, the jovial Toine still provided them with amusement. He would have made the devil himself laugh. Three men were regular in their attendance at the bedside: Celestin Maloisel, a tall, thin fellow, somewhat gnarled, like the trunk of an apple-tree; Prosper Horslaville, a withered little man with a ferret nose, cunning as a fox; and Cesaire Paumelle, who never spoke, but who enjoyed Toine's society all the same.

They brought a plank from the yard, propped it upon the edge of the bed, and played dominoes from two till six.

But Toine's wife soon became insufferable. She could not endure that her fat, lazy husband should amuse himself at games while lying in his bed; and whenever she caught him beginning a game she pounced furiously on the dominoes, overturned the plank, and carried all away into the bar, declaring that it was quite enough to have to feed that fat, lazy pig without seeing him amusing himself, as if to annoy poor people who had to work hard all day long.

Celestin Maloisel and Cesaire Paumelle bent their heads to the storm, but Prosper Horslaville egged on the old woman, and was only amused at her wrath.

One day, when she was more angry than usual, he said:

"Do you know what I'd do if I were you?"

She fixed her owl's eyes on him, and waited for his next words. Prosper went on:

"Your man is as hot as an oven, and he never leaves his bed—well, I'd make him hatch some eggs."

She was struck dumb at the suggestion, thinking that Prosper could not possibly be in earnest. But he continued:

"I'd put five under one arm, and five under the other, the same day that I set a hen. They'd all come out at the same time; then I'd take your husband's chickens to the hen to bring up with her own. You'd rear a fine lot that way."

"Could it be done?" asked the astonished old woman.

"Could it be done?" echoed the man. "Why not? Since eggs can be hatched in a warm box why shouldn't they be hatched in a warm bed?"

She was struck by this reasoning, and went away soothed and reflective.

A week later she entered Toine's room with her apron full of eggs, and said:

"I've just put the yellow hen on ten eggs. Here are ten for you; try not to break them."

"What do you want?" asked the amazed Toine.

"I want you to hatch them, you lazy creature!" she answered.

He laughed at first; then, finding she was serious, he got angry, and refused absolutely to have the eggs put under his great arms, that the warmth of his body might hatch them.

But the old woman declared wrathfully:

"You'll get no dinner as long as you won't have them. You'll see what'll happen."

Tome was uneasy, but answered nothing.

When twelve o'clock struck, he called out:

"Hullo, mother, is the soup ready?"

"There's no soup for you, lazy-bones," cried the old woman from her kitchen.

He thought she must be joking, and waited a while. Then he begged, implored, swore, "tacked to the north" and "tacked to the south," and beat on the wall with his fists, but had to consent at last to five eggs being placed against his left side; after which he had his soup.

When his friends arrived that afternoon they thought he must be ill, he seemed so constrained and queer.

They started the daily game of dominoes. But Tome appeared to take no pleasure in it, and reached forth his hand very slowly, and with great precaution.

"What's wrong with your arm?" asked Horslaville.

"I have a sort of stiffness in the shoulder," answered Toine.

Suddenly they heard people come into the inn. The players were silent.

It was the mayor with the deputy. They ordered two glasses of Extra-Special, and began to discuss local affairs. As they were talking in somewhat low tones Toine wanted to put his ear to the wall, and, forgetting all about his eggs, he made a sudden "tack to the north," which had the effect of plunging him into the midst of an omelette.

At the loud oath he swore his wife came hurrying into the room, and, guessing what had happened, stripped the bedclothes from him with lightning rapidity. She stood at first without moving or uttering a syllable, speechless with indignation at sight of the yellow poultice sticking to her husband's side.

Then, trembling with fury, she threw herself on the paralytic, showering on him blows such as those with which she cleaned her linen on the seashore. Tome's three friends were choking with laughter, coughing, spluttering and shouting, and the fat innkeeper himself warded his wife's attacks with all the prudence of which he was capable, that he might not also break the five eggs at his other side.

Tome was conquered. He had to hatch eggs, he had to give up his games of dominoes and renounce movement of any sort, for the old woman angrily deprived him of food whenever he broke an egg.

He lay on his back, with eyes fixed on the ceiling, motionless, his arms raised like wings, warming against his body the rudimentary chickens enclosed in their white shells.

He spoke now only in hushed tones; as if he feared a noise as much as motion, and he took a feverish interest in the yellow hen who was accomplishing in the poultry-yard the same task as he.

"Has the yellow hen eaten her food all right?" he would ask his wife.

And the old woman went from her fowls to her husband and from her husband to her fowls, devoured by anxiety as to the welfare of the little chickens who were maturing in the bed and in the nest.

The country people who knew the story came, agog with curiosity, to ask news of Toine. They entered his room on tiptoe, as one enters a sick-chamber, and asked:

"Well! how goes it?"

"All right," said Toine; "only it keeps me fearfully hot."

One morning his wife entered in a state of great excitement, and declared:

"The yellow hen has seven chickens! Three of the eggs were addled."

Toine's heart beat painfully. How many would he have?

"Will it soon be over?" he asked, with the anguish of a woman who is about to become a mother.

"It's to be hoped so!" answered the old woman crossly, haunted by fear of failure.

They waited. Friends of Toine who had got wind that his time was drawing near arrived, and filled the little room.

Nothing else was talked about in the neighboring cottages. Inquirers asked one another for news as they stood at their doors.

About three o'clock Toine fell asleep. He slumbered half his time nowadays. He was suddenly awakened by an unaccustomed tickling under his right arm. He put his left hand on the spot, and seized a little creature covered with yellow down, which fluttered in his hand.

His emotion was so great that he cried out, and let go his hold of the chicken, which ran over his chest. The bar was full of people at the time. The customers rushed to Toine's room, and made a circle round him as they would round a travelling showman; while Madame Toine picked up the chicken, which had taken refuge under her husband's beard.

No one spoke, so great was the tension. It was a warm April day. Outside the window the yellow hen could be heard calling to her newly-fledged brood.

Toine, who was perspiring with emotion and anxiety, murmured:

"I have another now—under the left arm."

His' wife plunged her great bony hand into the bed, and pulled out a second chicken with all the care of a midwife.

The neighbors wanted to see it. It was passed from one to another, and examined as if it were a phenomenon.

For twenty minutes no more hatched out, then four emerged at the same moment from their shells.

There was a great commotion among the lookers-on. And Toine smiled with satisfaction, beginning to take pride in this unusual sort of paternity. There were not many like him! Truly, he was a remarkable specimen of humanity!

"That makes six!" he declared. "Great heavens, what a christening we'll have!"

And a loud laugh rose from all present. Newcomers filled the bar. They asked one another:

"How many are there?"

"Six."

Toine's wife took this new family to the hen, who clucked loudly, bristled her feathers, and spread her wings wide to shelter her growing brood of little ones.

"There's one more!" cried Toine.

He was mistaken. There were three! It was an unalloyed triumph! The last chicken broke through its shell at seven o'clock in the evening. All the eggs were good! And Toine, beside himself with joy, his brood hatched out, exultant, kissed the tiny creature on the back, almost suffocating it. He wanted to keep it in his bed until morning, moved by a mother's tenderness toward the tiny being which he had brought to life, but the old woman carried it away like the others, turning a deaf ear to her husband's entreaties.

The delighted spectators went off to spread the news of the event, and Horslaville, who was the last to go, asked:

"You'll invite me when the first is cooked, won't you, Toine?"

At this idea a smile overspread the fat man's face, and he answered:

"Certainly I'll invite you, my son-in-law."

MADAME HUSSON'S "ROSIER"

We had just left Gisors, where I was awakened to hearing the name of the town called out by the guards, and I was dozing off again when a terrific shock threw me forward on top of a large lady who sat opposite me.

One of the wheels of the engine had broken, and the engine itself lay across the track. The tender and the baggage car were also derailed, and lay beside this mutilated engine, which rattled, groaned, hissed, puffed, sputtered, and resembled those horses that fall in the street with their flanks heaving, their breast palpitating, their nostrils steaming and their whole body trembling, but incapable of the slightest effort to rise and start off again.

There were no dead or wounded; only a few with bruises, for the train was not going at full speed. And we looked with sorrow at the great crippled iron creature that could not draw us along any more, and that blocked the track, perhaps for some time, for no doubt they would have to send to Paris for a special train to come to our aid.

It was then ten o'clock in the morning, and I at once decided to go back to Gisors for breakfast.

As I was walking along I said to myself:

"Gisors, Gisors—why, I know someone there!

"Who is it? Gisors? Let me see, I have a friend in this town." A name suddenly came to my mind, "Albert Marambot." He was an old school friend whom I had not seen for at least twelve years, and who was practicing medicine in Gisors. He had often written, inviting me to come and see him, and I had always promised to do so, without keeping my word. But at last I would take advantage of this opportunity.

I asked the first passer-by:

"Do you know where Dr. Marambot lives?"

He replied, without hesitation, and with the drawling accent of the Normans:

"Rue Dauphine."

I presently saw, on the door of the house he pointed out, a large brass plate on which was engraved the name of my old chum. I rang the bell, but the servant, a yellow-haired girl who moved slowly, said with a Stupid air:

"He isn't here, he isn't here."

I heard a sound of forks and of glasses and I cried:

"Hallo, Marambot!"

A door opened and a large man, with whiskers and a cross look on his face, appeared, carrying a dinner napkin in his hand.

I certainly should not have recognized him. One would have said he was forty-five at least, and, in a second, all the provincial life which makes one grow heavy, dull and old came before me. In a single flash of thought, quicker than the act of extending my hand to him, I could see his life, his manner of existence, his line of thought and his theories of things in general. I guessed at the prolonged meals that had rounded out his stomach, his after-dinner naps from the torpor of a slow indigestion aided by cognac, and his vague glances cast on the patient while he thought of the chicken that was roasting before the fire. His conversations about cooking, about cider, brandy and wine, the way of preparing certain dishes and of blending certain sauces were revealed to me at sight of his puffy red cheeks, his heavy lips and his lustreless eyes.

"You do not recognize me. I am Raoul Aubertin," I said.

He opened his arms and gave me such a hug that I thought he would choke me.

"You have not breakfasted, have you?"

"No."

"How fortunate! I was just sitting down to table and I have an excellent trout."

Five minutes later I was sitting opposite him at breakfast. I said:

"Are you a bachelor?"

"Yes, indeed."

"And do you like it here?"

"Time does not hang heavy; I am busy. I have patients and friends. I eat well, have good health, enjoy laughing and shooting. I get along."

"Is not life very monotonous in this little town?"

"No, my dear boy, not when one knows how to fill in the time. A little town, in fact, is like a large one. The incidents and amusements are less varied, but one makes more of them; one has fewer acquaintances, but one meets them more frequently. When you know all the windows in a street, each one of them interests you and puzzles you more than a whole street in Paris.

"A little town is very amusing, you know, very amusing, very amusing. Why, take Gisors. I know it at the tips of my fingers, from its beginning up to the present time. You have no idea what queer history it has."

"Do you belong to Gisors?"

"I? No. I come from Gournay, its neighbor and rival. Gournay is to Gisors what Lucullus was to Cicero. Here, everything is for glory; they say 'the proud people of Gisors.' At Gournay, everything is for the stomach; they say 'the chewers of Gournay.' Gisors despises Gournay, but Gournay laughs at Gisors. It is a very comical country, this."

I perceived that I was eating something very delicious, hard-boiled eggs wrapped in a covering of meat jelly flavored with herbs and put on ice for a few moments. I said as I smacked my lips to compliment Marambot:

"That is good."

He smiled.

"Two things are necessary, good jelly, which is hard to get, and good eggs. Oh, how rare good eggs are, with the yolks slightly reddish, and with a good flavor! I have two poultry yards, one for eggs and the other for chickens. I feed my laying hens in a special manner. I have my own ideas on the subject. In an egg, as in the meat of a chicken, in beef, or in mutton, in milk, in everything, one perceives, and ought to taste, the juice, the quintessence of all the food on which the animal has fed. How much better food we could have if more attention were paid to this!"

I laughed as I said:

"You are a gourmand?"

"Parbleu. It is only imbeciles who are not. One is a gourmand as one is an artist, as one is learned, as one is a poet. The sense of taste, my friend, is very delicate, capable of perfection, and quite as worthy of respect as the eye and the ear. A person who lacks this sense is deprived of an exquisite faculty, the faculty of discerning the quality of food, just as one may lack the faculty of discerning the beauties of a book or of a work of art; it means to be deprived of an essential organ, of something that belongs to higher humanity; it means to belong to one of those innumerable classes of the infirm, the unfortunate, and the fools of which our race is composed; it means to have the mouth of an animal, in a word, just like the mind of an animal. A man who cannot distinguish one kind of lobster from another; a herring—that admirable fish that has all the flavors, all the odors of the sea—from a mackerel or a whiting; and a Cresane from a Duchess pear, may be compared to a man who should mistake Balzac for Eugene Sue; a symphony of Beethoven for a military march composed by the bandmaster of a regiment; and the Apollo Belvidere for the statue of General de Blaumont.

"Who is General de Blaumont?"

"Oh, that's true, you do not know. It is easy to tell that you do not belong to Gisors. I told you just now, my dear boy, that they called the inhabitants of this town 'the proud people of Gisors,' and never was an epithet better deserved. But let us finish breakfast first, and then I will tell you about our town and take you to see it."

He stopped talking every now and then while he slowly drank a glass of wine which he gazed at affectionately as he replaced the glass on the table.

It was amusing to see him, with a napkin tied around his neck, his cheeks flushed, his eyes eager, and his whiskers spreading round his mouth as it kept working.

He made me eat until I was almost choking. Then, as I was about to return to the railway station, he seized me by the arm and took me through the streets. The town, of a pretty, provincial type, commanded by its citadel, the most curious monument of military architecture of the seventh century to be found in France, overlooks, in its turn, a long, green valley, where the large Norman cows graze and ruminate in the pastures.

The doctor quoted:

"'Gisors, a town of 4,000 inhabitants in the department of Eure, mentioned in Caesar's Commentaries: Caesaris ostium, then Caesartium, Caesortium, Gisortium, Gisors.' I shall not take you to visit the old Roman encampment, the remains of which are still in existence."

I laughed and replied:

"My dear friend, it seems to me that you are affected with a special malady that, as a doctor, you ought to study; it is called the spirit of provincialism."

He stopped abruptly.

"The spirit of provincialism, my friend, is nothing but natural patriotism," he said. "I love my house, my town and my province because I discover in them the customs of my own village; but if I love my country, if I become angry when a neighbor sets foot in it, it is because I feel that my home is in danger, because the frontier that I do not know is the high road to my province. For instance, I am a Norman, a true Norman; well, in spite of my hatred of the German and my desire for revenge, I do not detest them, I do

not hate them by instinct as I hate the English, the real, hereditary natural enemy of the Normans; for the English traversed this
soil inhabited by my ancestors, plundered and ravaged it twenty
times, and my aversion to this perfidious people was transmitted
to me at birth by my father. See, here is the statue of the general."

"What general?"

"General Blaumont! We had to have a statue. We are not 'the
proud people of Gisors' for nothing! So we discovered General de
Blaumont. Look in this bookseller's window."

He drew me towards the bookstore, where about fifteen red,
yellow and blue volumes attracted the eye. As I read the titles, I
began to laugh idiotically. They read:

Gisors, its origin, its future, by M. X. . . ., member of several
learned societies; History of Gisors, by the Abbe A . . .; Gisors
from the time of Caesar to the present day, by M. B. . . ., Land-
owner; Gisors and its environs, by Doctor C. D. . . .; The Glories of
Gisors, by a Discoverer.

"My friend," resumed Marambot, "not a year, not a single year,
you understand, passes without a fresh history of Gisors being
published here; we now have twenty-three."

"And the glories of Gisors?" I asked.

"Oh, I will not mention them all, only the principal ones. We had
first General de Blaumont, then Baron Davillier, the celebrated
ceramist who explored Spain and the Balearic Isles, and brought
to the notice of collectors the wonderful Hispano-Arabic china.
In literature we have a very clever journalist, now dead, Charles
Brainne, and among those who are living, the very eminent edi-
tor of the Nouvelliste de Rouen, Charles Lapierre . . . and many
others, many others."

We were traversing along street with a gentle incline, with a
June sun beating down on it and driving the residents into their
houses.

Suddenly there appeared at the farther end of the street a drunk-
en man who was staggering along, with his head forward his
arms and legs limp. He would walk forward rapidly three, six, or
ten steps and then stop. When these energetic movements landed
him in the middle of the road he stopped short and swayed on his
feet, hesitating between falling and a fresh start. Then he would
dart off in any direction, sometimes falling against the wall of
a house, against which he seemed to be fastened, as though he
were trying to get in through the wall. Then he would suddenly turn round and look ahead of him, his mouth open and his
eyes blinking in the sunlight, and getting away from the wall by

a movement of the hips, he started off once more.

A little yellow dog, a half-starved cur, followed him, barking; stopping when he stopped, and starting off when he started.

"Hallo," said Marambot, "there is Madame Husson's 'Rosier'.

"Madame Husson's 'Rosier'," I exclaimed in astonishment. "What do you mean?"

The doctor began to laugh.

"Oh, that is what we call drunkards round here. The name comes from an old story which has now become a legend, although it is true in all respects."

"Is it an amusing story?"

"Very amusing."

"Well, then, tell it to me."

"I will."

There lived formerly in this town a very upright old lady who was a great guardian of morals and was called Mme. Husson. You know, I am telling you the real names and not imaginary ones. Mme. Husson took a special interest in good works, in helping the poor and encouraging the deserving. She was a little woman with a quick walk and wore a black wig. She was ceremonious, polite, on very good terms with the Almighty in the person of Abby Malon, and had a profound horror, an inborn horror of vice, and, in particular, of the vice the Church calls lasciviousness. Any irregularity before marriage made her furious, exasperated her till she was beside herself.

Now, this was the period when they presented a prize as a reward of virtue to any girl in the environs of Paris who was found to be chaste. She was called a Rosiere, and Mme. Husson got the idea that she would institute a similar ceremony at Gisors. She spoke about it to Abbe Malon, who at once made out a list of candidates.

However, Mme. Husson had a servant, an old woman called Francoise, as upright as her mistress. As soon as the priest had left, madame called the servant and said:

"Here, Francoise, here are the girls whose names M. le cure has submitted to me for the prize of virtue; try and find out what reputation they bear in the district."

And Francoise set out. She collected all the scandal, all the stories, all the tattle, all the suspicions. That she might omit nothing, she wrote it all down together with her memoranda in her housekeeping book, and handed it each morning to Mme. Husson, who, after adjusting her spectacles on her thin nose, read as follows:

Bread...........................*four sous*
Milk............................*two sous*
Butter ....*eight sous*

Malvina Levesque got into trouble last year with Mathurin Poilu.

Leg of mutton...................*twenty-five sous*
Salt............................*one sou*

Rosalie Vatinel was seen in the Riboudet woods with Cesaire Pienoir, by

Mme. Onesime, the ironer, on July the 20th about dusk.

Radishes........................*one sou*
Vinegar.........................*two sous*
Oxalic acid.....................*two sous*

Josephine Durdent, who is not believed to have committed a fault, although she corresponds with young Oportun, who is in service in Rouen, and who sent her a present of a cap by diligence.

Not one came out unscathed in this rigorous inquisition. Francoise inquired of everyone, neighbors, drapers, the principal, the teaching sisters at school, and gathered the slightest details.

As there is not a girl in the world about whom gossips have not found something to say, there was not found in all the countryside one young girl whose name was free from some scandal.

But Mme. Husson desired that the "Rosiere" of Gisors, like Caesar's wife, should be above suspicion, and she was horrified, saddened and in despair at the record in her servant's housekeeping account-book.

They then extended their circle of inquiries to the neighboring villages; but with no satisfaction.

They consulted the mayor. His candidates failed. Those of Dr. Barbesol were equally unlucky, in spite of the exactness of his scientific vouchers.

But one morning Francoise, on returning from one of her expeditions, said to her mistress:

"You see, madame, that if you wish to give a prize to anyone, there is only Isidore in all the country round."

Mme. Husson remained thoughtful. She knew him well, this Isidore, the son of Virginie the greengrocer. His proverbial virtue had been the delight of Gisors for several years, and served as an entertaining theme of conversation in the town, and of amusement to the young girls who loved to tease him. He was past twenty-one, was tall, awkward, slow and timid; helped his mother in the business, and spent his days picking over fruit and vegetables, seated on a chair outside the door.

He had an abnormal dread of a petticoat and cast down his eyes whenever a female customer looked at him smilingly, and this well-known timidity made him the butt of all the wags in the country.

Bold words, coarse expressions, indecent allusions, brought the color to his cheeks so quickly that Dr. Barbesol had nicknamed him "the thermometer of modesty." Was he as innocent as he looked? ill-natured people asked themselves. Was it the mere presentiment of unknown and shameful mysteries or else indignation at the relations ordained as the concomitant of love that so strongly affected the son of Virginie the greengrocer? The urchins of the neighborhood as they ran past the shop would fling disgusting remarks at him just to see him cast down his eyes. The girls amused themselves by walking up and down before him, cracking jokes that made him go into the store. The boldest among them teased him to his face just to have a laugh, to amuse themselves, made appointments with him and proposed all sorts of things.

So Madame Husson had become thoughtful.

Certainly, Isidore was an exceptional case of notorious, unassailable virtue. No one, among the most sceptical, most incredulous, would have been able, would have dared, to suspect Isidore of the slightest infraction of any law of morality. He had never been seen in a cafe, never been seen at night on the street. He went to bed at eight o'clock and rose at four. He was a perfection, a pearl.

But Mme. Husson still hesitated. The idea of substituting a boy for a girl, a "rosier" for a "rosiere," troubled her, worried her a little, and she resolved to consult Abbe Malon.

The abbe responded:

"What do you desire to reward, madame? It is virtue, is it not, and nothing but virtue? What does it matter to you, therefore, if it is masculine or feminine? Virtue is eternal; it has neither sex nor country; it is 'Virtue.'"

Thus encouraged, Mme. Husson went to see the mayor.

He approved heartily.

"We will have a fine ceremony," he said. "And another year if we can find a girl as worthy as Isidore we will give the reward to her. It will even be a good example that we shall set to Nanterre. Let us not be exclusive; let us welcome all merit."

Isidore, who had been told about this, blushed deeply and seemed happy.

The ceremony was fixed for the 15th of August, the festival of the Virgin Mary and of the Emperor Napoleon. The municipality had decided to make an imposing ceremony and had built the platform on the couronneaux, a delightful extension of the ramparts of the old citadel where I will take you presently.

With the natural revulsion of public feeling, the virtue of Isidore, ridiculed hitherto, had suddenly become respected and envied, as it would bring him in five hundred francs besides a savings bank book, a mountain of consideration, and glory enough and to spare. The girls now regretted their frivolity, their ridicule, their bold manners; and Isidore, although still modest and timid, had now a little contented air that bespoke his internal satisfaction.

The evening before the 15th of August the entire Rue Dauphine was decorated with flags. Oh, I forgot to tell you why this street had been called Rue Dauphine.

It seems that the wife or mother of the dauphin, I do not remember which one, while visiting Gisors had been feted so much by the authorities that during a triumphal procession through the town she stopped before one of the houses in this street, halting the procession, and exclaimed:

"Oh, the pretty house! How I should like to go through it! To whom does it belong?"

They told her the name of the owner, who was sent for and brought, proud and embarrassed, before the princess. She alighted from her carriage, went into the house, wishing to go over it from top to bottom, and even shut herself in one of the rooms alone for a few seconds.

When she came out, the people, flattered at this honor paid to a citizen of Gisors, shouted "Long live the dauphine!" But a rhymester wrote some words to a refrain, and the street retained the title of her royal highness, for

"The princess, in a hurry,
Without bell, priest, or beadle,
But with some water only,
Had baptized it."

But to come back to Isidore.

They had scattered flowers all along the road as they do for processions at the Fete-Dieu, and the National Guard was present, acting on the orders of their chief, Commandant Desbarres, an old soldier of the Grand Army, who pointed with pride to the beard of a Cossack cut with a single sword stroke from the chin of its owner by the commandant during the retreat in Russia, and which hung beside the frame containing the cross of the Legion of Honor presented to him by the emperor himself.

The regiment that he commanded was, besides, a picked regiment celebrated all through the province, and the company of grenadiers of Gisors was called on to attend all important ceremonies for a distance of fifteen to twenty leagues. The story goes that Louis Philippe, while reviewing the militia of Eure, stopped in astonishment before the company from Gisors, exclaiming:

"Oh, who are those splendid grenadiers?"

"The grenadiers of Gisors," replied the general.

"I might have known it," murmured the king.

So Commandant Desbarres came at the head of his men, preceded by the band, to get Isidore in his mother's store.

After a little air had been played by the band beneath the windows, the "Rosier" himself appeared—on the threshold. He was dressed in white duck from head to foot and wore a straw hat with a little bunch of orange blossoms as a cockade.

The question of his clothes had bothered Mme. Husson a good deal, and she hesitated some time between the black coat of those who make their first communion and an entire white suit. But Francoise, her counsellor, induced her to decide on the white suit, pointing out that the Rosier would look like a swan.

Behind him came his guardian, his godmother, Mme. Husson, in triumph. She took his arm to go out of the store, and the mayor placed himself on the other side of the Rosier. The drums beat. Commandant Desbarres gave the order "Present arms!" The procession resumed its march towards the church amid an immense crowd of people who has gathered from the neighboring districts.

After a short mass and an affecting discourse by Abbe Malon, they continued on their way to the couronneaux, where the banquet was served in a tent.

Before taking their seats at table, the mayor gave an address. This is it, word for word. I learned it by heart:

"Young man, a woman of means, beloved by the poor and respected by the rich, Mme. Husson, whom the whole country is thanking here, through me, had the idea, the happy and benevolent idea, of founding in this town a prize for virtue, which should serve as a valuable encouragement to the inhabitants of this beautiful country.

"You, young man, are the first to be rewarded in this dynasty of goodness and chastity. Your name will remain at the head of this list of the most deserving, and your life, understand me, your whole life, must correspond to this happy commencement. To-day, in presence of this noble woman, of these soldier-citizens who have taken up their arms in your honor, in presence of this populace, affected, assembled to applaud you, or, rather, to applaud virtue, in your person, you make a solemn contract with the town, with all of us, to continue until your death the excellent example of your youth.

"Do not forget, young man, that you are the first seed cast into this field of hope; give us the fruits that we expect of you."

The mayor advanced three steps, opened his arms and pressed Isidore to his heart.

The "Rosier" was sobbing without knowing why, from a confused emotion, from pride and a vague and happy feeling of tenderness.

Then the mayor placed in one hand a silk purse in which gold tingled —five hundred francs in gold!—and in his other hand a savings bank book. And he said in a solemn tone:

"Homage, glory and riches to virtue."

Commandant Desbarres shouted "Bravo!" the grenadiers vociferated, and the crowd applauded.

Mme. Husson wiped her eyes, in her turn. Then they all sat down at the table where the banquet was served.

The repast was magnificent and seemed interminable. One course followed another; yellow cider and red wine in fraternal contact blended in the stomach of the guests. The rattle of plates, the sound of voices, and of music softly played, made an incessant deep hum, and was dispersed abroad in the clear sky where the swallows were flying. Mme. Husson occasionally readjusted her black wig, which would slip over on one side, and chatted with Abbe Malon. The mayor, who was excited, talked politics with Commandant Desbarres, and Isidore ate, drank, as if he had never eaten or drunk before. He helped himself repeatedly to all the dishes, becoming aware for the first time of the pleasure of having one's belly full of good things which tickle the palate in the first place. He had let out a reef in his belt and, without speaking, and although he was a little uneasy at a wine stain on his white waistcoat, he ceased eating in order to take up his glass and hold it to his mouth as long as possible, to enjoy the taste slowly.

It was time for the toasts. They were many and loudly applauded. Evening was approaching and they had been at the table since noon. Fine, milky vapors were already floating in the air in the valley, the light night-robe of streams and meadows; the sun neared the horizon; the cows were lowing in the distance amid the mists of the pasture. The feast was over. They returned to Gisors. The procession, now disbanded, walked in detachments. Mme. Husson had taken Isidore's arm and was giving him a quantity of urgent, excellent advice.

They stopped at the door of the fruit store, and the "Rosier" was left at his mother's house. She had not come home yet. Having been invited by her family to celebrate her son's triumph, she had taken luncheon with her sister after having followed the procession as far as the banqueting tent.

So Isidore remained alone in the store, which was growing dark. He sat down on a chair, excited by the wine and by pride, and looked about him. Carrots, cabbages, and onions gave out their strong odor of vegetables in the closed room, that coarse smell of the garden blended with the sweet, penetrating odor of strawberries and the delicate, slight, evanescent fragrance of a basket of peaches.

The "Rosier" took one of these and ate it, although he was as full as an egg. Then, all at once, wild with joy, he began to dance about the store, and something rattled in his waistcoat.

He was surprised, and put his hand in his pocket and brought out the purse containing the five hundred francs, which he had forgotten in his agitation. Five hundred francs! What a fortune! He poured the gold pieces out on the counter and spread them out with his big hand with a slow, caressing touch so as to see them all at the same time. There were twenty-five, twenty-five round gold pieces, all gold! They glistened on the wood in the dim light and he counted them over and over, one by one. Then he put them back in the purse, which he replaced in his pocket.

Who will ever know or who can tell what a terrible conflict took place in the soul of the "Rosier" between good and evil, the tumultuous attack of Satan, his artifices, the temptations which he offered to this timid virgin heart? What suggestions, what imaginations, what desires were not invented by the evil one to excite and destroy this chosen one? He seized his hat, Mme. Husson's saint, his hat, which still bore the little bunch of orange blossoms, and going out through the alley at the back of the house, he disappeared in the darkness.

Virginie, the fruiterer, on learning that her son had returned, went home at once, and found the house empty. She waited, without thinking anything about it at first; but at the end of a quarter of an hour she made inquiries. The neighbors had seen Isidore come home and had not seen him go out again. They began to look for him, but could not find him. His mother, in alarm, went to the mayor. The mayor knew nothing, except that he had left him at the door of his home. Mme. Husson had just retired when they informed her that her protege had disappeared. She immediately put on her wig, dressed herself and went to Virginie's house. Virginie, whose plebeian soul was readily moved, was weeping copiously amid her cabbages, carrots and onions.

They feared some accident had befallen him. What could it be? Commandant Desbarres notified the police, who made a circuit of the town, and on the high road to Pontoise they found the little bunch of orange blossoms. It was placed on a table around which the authorities were deliberating. The "Rosier" must have been the victim of some stratagem, some trick, some jealousy; but in what way? What means had been employed to kidnap this innocent creature, and with what object?

Weary of looking for him without any result, Virginie, alone, remained watching and weeping.

The following evening, when the coach passed by on its return from Paris, Gisors learned with astonishment that its "Rosier" had stopped the vehicle at a distance of about two hundred metres from the town, had climbed up on it and paid his fare, handing over a gold piece and receiving the change, and that he had quietly alighted in the centre of the great city.

There was great excitement all through the countryside. Letters passed between the mayor and the chief of police in Paris, but brought no result.

The days followed one another, a week passed.

Now, one morning, Dr. Barbesol, who had gone out early, perceived, sitting on a doorstep, a man dressed in a grimy linen suit, who was sleeping with his head leaning against the wall. He approached him and recognized Isidore. He tried to rouse him, but did not succeed in doing so. The ex-"Rosier" was in that profound, invincible sleep that is alarming, and the doctor, in surprise, went to seek assistance to help him in carrying the young man to Boncheval's drugstore. When they lifted him up they found an empty bottle under him, and when the doctor sniffed at it, he declared that it had contained brandy. That gave a suggestion as to what treatment he would require. They succeeded in rousing him.

Isidore was drunk, drunk and degraded by a week of guzzling, drunk and so disgusting that a ragman would not have touched him. His beautiful white duck suit was a gray rag, greasy, muddy, torn, and destroyed, and he smelt of the gutter and of vice.

He was washed, sermonized, shut up, and did not leave the house for four days. He seemed ashamed and repentant. They could not find on him either his purse, containing the five hundred francs, or the bankbook, or even his silver watch, a sacred heirloom left by his father, the fruiterer.

On the fifth day he ventured into the Rue Dauphine, Curious glances followed him and he walked along with a furtive expression in his eyes and his head bent down. As he got outside the town towards the valley they lost sight of him; but two hours later he returned laughing and rolling against the walls. He was drunk, absolutely drunk.

Nothing could cure him.

Driven from home by his mother, he became a wagon driver, and drove the charcoal wagons for the Pougrisel firm, which is still in existence.

His reputation as a drunkard became so well known and spread so far that even at Evreux they talked of Mme. Husson's "Rosier," and the sots of the countryside have been given that nickname.

A good deed is never lost.

Dr. Marambot rubbed his hands as he finished his story. I asked: "Did you know the 'Rosier'?"

"Yes. I had the honor of closing his eyes."

"What did he die of?"

"An attack of delirium tremens, of course."

We had arrived at the old citadel, a pile of ruined walls dominated by the enormous tower of St. Thomas of Canterbury and the one called the Prisoner's Tower.

Marambot told me the story of this prisoner, who, with the aid of a nail, covered the walls of his dungeon with sculptures, tracing the reflections of the sun as it glanced through the narrow slit of a loophole.

I also learned that Clothaire II had given the patrimony of Gisors to his cousin, Saint Romain, bishop of Rouen; that Gisors ceased to be the capital of the whole of Vexin after the treaty of Saint-Clair-sur-Epte; that the town is the chief strategic centre of all that portion of France, and that in consequence of this advantage she was taken and retaken over and over again. At the command of William the Red, the eminent engineer, Robert de Bellesme, constructed there a powerful fortress that was attacked later by Louis le Gros, then by the Norman barons, was defended by Robert de Candos, was finally ceded to Louis le Gros by Geoffry Plantagenet, was retaken by the English in consequence of the treachery of the Knights-Templars, was contested by Philippe-Augustus and Richard the Lionhearted, was set on fire by Edward III of England, who could not take the castle, was again taken by the English in 1419, restored later to Charles VIII by Richard de Marbury, was taken by the Duke of Calabria occupied by the League, inhabited by Henry IV, etc., etc.

And Marambot, eager and almost eloquent, continued:

"What beggars, those English! And what sots, my boy; they are all 'Rosiers,' those hypocrites!"

Then, after a silence, stretching out his arm towards the tiny river that glistened in the meadows, he said:

"Did you know that Henry Monnier was one of the most untiring fishermen on the banks of the Epte?"

"No, I did not know it."

"And Bouffe, my boy, Bouffe was a painter on glass."

"You are joking!"

"No, indeed. How is it you do not know these things?"

THE ADOPTED SON

The two cottages stood beside each other at the foot of a hill near a little seashore resort. The two peasants labored hard on the unproductive soil to rear their little ones, and each family had four.

Before the adjoining doors a whole troop of urchins played and tumbled about from morning till night. The two eldest were six years old, and the youngest were about fifteen months; the marriages, and afterward the births, having taken place nearly simultaneously in both families.

The two mothers could hardly distinguish their own offspring among the lot, and as for the fathers, they were altogether at sea. The eight names danced in their heads; they were always getting them mixed up; and when they wished to call one child, the men often called three names before getting the right one.

The first of the two cottages, as you came up from the bathing beach, Rolleport, was occupied by the Tuvaches, who had three girls and one boy; the other house sheltered the Vallins, who had one girl and three boys.

They all subsisted frugally on soup, potatoes and fresh air. At seven o'clock in the morning, then at noon, then at six o'clock in the evening, the housewives got their broods together to give them their food, as the gooseherds collect their charges. The children were seated, according to age, before the wooden table, varnished by fifty years of use; the mouths of the youngest hardly reaching the level of the table. Before them was placed a bowl filled with bread, soaked in the water in which the potatoes had been boiled, half a cabbage and three onions; and the whole line ate until their hunger was appeased. The mother herself fed the smallest.

A small pot roast on Sunday was a feast for all; and the father on this day sat longer over the meal, repeating: "I wish we could have this every day."

One afternoon, in the month of August, a phaeton stopped suddenly in front of the cottages, and a young woman, who was driving the horses, said to the gentleman sitting at her side:

"Oh, look at all those children, Henri! How pretty they are, tumbling about in the dust, like that!"

The man did not answer, accustomed to these outbursts of admiration, which were a pain and almost a reproach to him. The young woman continued:

"I must hug them! Oh, how I should like to have one of them—that one there—the little tiny one!"

Springing down from the carriage, she ran toward the children, took one of the two youngest—a Tuvache child—and lifting it up in her arms, she kissed him passionately on his dirty cheeks, on his tousled hair daubed with earth, and on his little hands, with which he fought vigorously, to get away from the caresses which displeased him.

Then she got into the carriage again, and drove off at a lively trot. But she returned the following week, and seating herself on the ground, took the youngster in her arms, stuffed him with cakes; gave candies to all the others, and played with them like a young girl, while the husband waited patiently in the carriage.

She returned again; made the acquaintance of the parents, and reappeared every day with her pockets full of dainties and pennies.

Her name was Madame Henri d'Hubieres.

One morning, on arriving, her husband alighted with her, and without stopping to talk to the children, who now knew her well, she entered the farmer's cottage.

They were busy chopping wood for the fire. They rose to their feet in surprise, brought forward chairs, and waited expectantly.

Then the woman, in a broken, trembling voice, began:

"My good people, I have come to see you, because I should like—I should like to take—your little boy with me—"

The country people, too bewildered to think, did not answer.

She recovered her breath, and continued: "We are alone, my husband and I. We would keep it. Are you willing?"

The peasant woman began to understand. She asked:

"You want to take Charlot from us? Oh, no, indeed!"

Then M. d'Hubieres intervened:

"My wife has not made her meaning clear. We wish to adopt him, but he will come back to see you. If he turns out well, as there is every reason to expect, he will be our heir. If we, perchance, should have children, he will share equally with them; but if he should not reward our care, we should give him, when he comes of age, a sum of twenty thousand francs, which shall be deposited immediately in his name, with a lawyer. As we have thought also of you, we should pay you, until your death, a pension of one hundred francs a month. Do you understand me?"

The woman had arisen, furious.

"You want me to sell you Charlot? Oh, no, that's not the sort of thing to ask of a mother! Oh, no! That would be an abomination!"

The man, grave and deliberate, said nothing; but approved of what his wife said by a continued nodding of his head.

Madame d'Hubieres, in dismay, began to weep; turning to her husband, with a voice full of tears, the voice of a child used to having all its wishes gratified, she stammered:

"They will not do it, Henri, they will not do it."

Then he made a last attempt: "But, my friends, think of the child's future, of his happiness, of—"

The peasant woman, however, exasperated, cut him short:

"It's all considered! It's all understood! Get out of here, and don't let me see you again—the idea of wanting to take away a child like that!"

Madame d'Hubieres remembered that there were two children, quite little, and she asked, through her tears, with the tenacity of a wilful and spoiled woman:

"But is the other little one not yours?"

Father Tuvache answered: "No, it is our neighbors'. You can go to them if you wish." And he went back into his house, whence resounded the indignant voice of his wife.

The Vallins were at table, slowly eating slices of bread which they parsimoniously spread with a little rancid butter on a plate between the two.

M. d'Hubieres recommenced his proposals, but with more insinuations, more oratorical precautions, more shrewdness.

The two country people shook their heads, in sign of refusal, but when they learned that they were to have a hundred francs a month, they considered the matter, consulting one another by glances, much disturbed. They kept silent for a long time, tortured, hesitating. At last the woman asked: "What do you say to it, man?" In a weighty tone he said: "I say that it's not to be despised."

Madame d'Hubieres, trembling with anguish, spoke of the future of their child, of his happiness, and of the money which he could give them later.

The peasant asked: "This pension of twelve hundred francs, will it be promised before a lawyer?"

M. d'Hubieres responded: "Why, certainly, beginning with to-morrow."

The woman, who was thinking it over, continued:

"A hundred francs a month is not enough to pay for depriving us of the child. That child would be working in a few years; we must have a hundred and twenty francs."

Tapping her foot with impatience, Madame d'Hubieres granted it at once, and, as she wished to carry off the child with her, she gave a hundred francs extra, as a present, while her husband drew up a paper. And the young woman, radiant, carried off the howling brat, as one carries away a wished-for knick-knack from a shop.

The Tuvaches, from their door, watched her departure, silent, serious, perhaps regretting their refusal.

Nothing more was heard of little Jean Vallin. The parents went to the lawyer every month to collect their hundred and twenty francs. They had quarrelled with their neighbors, because Mother Tuvache grossly insulted them, continually, repeating from door to door that one must be unnatural to sell one's child; that it was horrible, disgusting, bribery. Sometimes she would take her Charlot in her arms, ostentatiously exclaiming, as if he understood:

"I didn't sell you, I didn't! I didn't sell you, my little one! I'm not rich, but I don't sell my children!"

The Vallins lived comfortably, thanks to the pension. That was the cause of the unappeasable fury of the Tuvaches, who had remained miserably poor. Their eldest went away to serve his time in the army; Charlot alone remained to labor with his old father, to support the mother and two younger sisters.

He had reached twenty-one years when, one morning, a brilliant carriage stopped before the two cottages. A young gentleman, with a gold watch-chain, got out, giving his hand to an aged, white-haired lady. The old lady said to him: "It is there, my child, at the second house." And he entered the house of the Vallins as though at home.

The old mother was washing her aprons; the infirm father slumbered at the chimney-corner. Both raised their heads, and the young man said:

"Good-morning, papa; good-morning, mamma!"

They both stood up, frightened! In a flutter, the peasant woman dropped her soap into the water, and stammered:

"Is it you, my child? Is it you, my child?"

He took her in his arms and hugged her, repeating: "Good-morning, mamma," while the old man, all a-tremble, said, in his calm tone which he never lost: "Here you are, back again, Jean," as if he had just seen him a month ago.

When they had got to know one another again, the parents wished to take their boy out in the neighborhood, and show him. They took him to the mayor, to the deputy, to the cure, and to the schoolmaster.

Charlot, standing on the threshold of his cottage, watched him pass. In the evening, at supper, he said to the old people: "You must have been stupid to let the Vallins' boy be taken."

The mother answered, obstinately: "I wouldn't sell my child."

The father remained silent. The son continued:

"It is unfortunate to be sacrificed like that."

Then Father Tuvache, in an angry tone, said:

"Are you going to reproach us for having kept you?" And the young man said, brutally:

"Yes, I reproach you for having been such fools. Parents like you make the misfortune of their children. You deserve that I should leave you." The old woman wept over her plate. She moaned, as she swallowed the spoonfuls of soup, half of which she spilled: "One may kill one's self to bring up children!"

Then the boy said, roughly: "I'd rather not have been born than be what I am. When I saw the other, my heart stood still. I said to myself: 'See what I should have been now!'" He got up: "See here, I feel that I would do better not to stay here, because I would throw it up to you from morning till night, and I would make your life miserable. I'll never forgive you for that!"

The two old people were silent, downcast, in tears.

He continued: "No, the thought of that would be too much. I'd rather look for a living somewhere else."

He opened the door. A sound of voices came in at the door. The Vallins were celebrating the return of their child.

COWARD

*I*n society he was called "Handsome Signoles." His name was Vicomte Gontran-Joseph de Signoles.

An orphan, and possessed of an ample fortune, he cut quite a dash, as it is called. He had an attractive appearance and manner, could talk well, had a certain inborn elegance, an air of pride and nobility, a good mustache, and a tender eye, that always finds favor with women.

He was in great request at receptions, waltzed to perfection, and was regarded by his own sex with that smiling hostility accorded to the popular society man. He had been suspected of more than one love affair, calculated to enhance the reputation of a bachelor. He lived a happy, peaceful life—a life of physical and mental well-being. He had won considerable fame as a swordsman, and still more as a marksman.

"When the time comes for me to fight a duel," he said, "I shall choose pistols. With such a weapon I am sure to kill my man."

One evening, having accompanied two women friends of his with their husbands to the theatre, he invited them to take some ice cream at Tortoni's after the performance. They had been seated a few minutes in the restaurant when Signoles noticed that a man was staring persistently at one of the ladies. She seemed annoyed, and lowered her eyes. At last she said to her husband:

"There's a man over there looking at me. I don't know him; do you?"

The husband, who had noticed nothing, glanced across at the offender, and said:

"No; not in the least."

His wife continued, half smiling, half angry:

"It's very tiresome! He quite spoils my ice cream."

The husband shrugged his shoulders.

"Nonsense! Don't take any notice of him. If we were to bother our heads about all the ill-mannered people we should have no time for anything else."

But the vicomte abruptly left his seat. He could not allow this insolent fellow to spoil an ice for a guest of his. It was for him to take cognizance of the offence, since it was through him that his friends had come to the restaurant. He went across to the man and said:

"Sir, you are staring at those ladies in a manner I cannot permit. I must ask you to desist from your rudeness."

The other replied:

"Let me alone, will you!"

"Take care, sir," said the vicomte between his teeth, "or you will force me to extreme measures."

The man replied with a single word—a foul word, which could be heard from one end of the restaurant to the other, and which startled every one there. All those whose backs were toward the two disputants turned round; all the others raised their heads; three waiters spun round on their heels like tops; the two lady cashiers jumped, as if shot, then turned their bodies simultaneously, like two automata worked by the same spring.

There was dead silence. Then suddenly a sharp, crisp sound. The vicomte had slapped his adversary's face. Every one rose to interfere. Cards were exchanged.

When the vicomte reached home he walked rapidly up and down his room for some minutes. He was in a state of too great agitation to think connectedly. One idea alone possessed him: a duel. But this idea aroused in him as yet no emotion of any kind. He had done what he was bound to do; he had proved himself to be what he ought to be. He would be talked about, approved, congratulated. He repeated aloud, speaking as one does when under the stress of great mental disturbance:

"What a brute of a man!" Then he sat down, and began to reflect. He would have to find seconds as soon as morning came. Whom should he choose? He bethought himself of the most influential and best-known men of his acquaintance. His choice fell at last on the Marquis de la Tour-Noire and Colonel Bourdin-a nobleman and a soldier. That would be just the thing. Their names would carry weight in the newspapers. He was thirsty, and drank three glasses of water, one after another; then he walked up and down again. If he showed himself brave, determined, prepared to face a duel in deadly earnest, his adversary would probably draw back and proffer excuses. He picked up the card he had taken from his pocket and thrown on a table. He read it again, as he had already read it, first at a glance in the restaurant, and afterward on the way home in the light of each gas lamp: "Georges Lamil, 51 Rue Moncey." That was all.

He examined closely this collection of letters, which seemed to him mysterious, fraught with many meanings. Georges Lamil! Who was the man? What was his profession? Why had he stared so at the woman? Was it not monstrous that a stranger, an unknown, should thus all at once upset one's whole life, simply because it had pleased him to stare rudely at a woman? And the vicomte once more repeated aloud:

"What a brute!"

Then he stood motionless, thinking, his eyes still fixed on the card. Anger rose in his heart against this scrap of paper—a resentful anger, mingled with a strange sense of uneasiness. It was a stupid business altogether! He took up a penknife which lay open within reach, and deliberately stuck it into the middle of the printed name, as if he were stabbing some one.

So he would have to fight! Should he choose swords or pistols?—for he considered himself as the insulted party. With the sword he would risk less, but with the pistol there was some chance of his adversary backing out. A duel with swords is rarely fatal, since mutual prudence prevents the combatants from fighting close enough to each other for a point to enter very deep. With pistols he would seriously risk his life; but, on the other hand, he might come out of the affair with flying colors, and without a duel, after all.

"I must be firm," he said. "The fellow will be afraid."

The sound of his own voice startled him, and he looked nervously round the room. He felt unstrung. He drank another glass of water, and then began undressing, preparatory to going to bed.

As soon as he was in bed he blew out the light and shut his eyes.

"I have all day to-morrow," he reflected, "for setting my affairs in order. I must sleep now, in order to be calm when the time comes."

He was very warm in bed, but he could not succeed in losing consciousness. He tossed and turned, remained for five minutes lying on his back, then changed to his left side, then rolled over to his right. He was thirsty again, and rose to drink. Then a qualm seized him:

"Can it be possible that I am afraid?"

Why did his heart beat so uncontrollably at every well-known sound in his room? When the clock was about to strike, the prefatory grating of its spring made him start, and for several seconds he panted for breath, so unnerved was he.

He began to reason with himself on the possibility of such a thing: "Could I by any chance be afraid?"

No, indeed; he could not be afraid, since he was resolved to proceed to the last extremity, since he was irrevocably determined to fight without flinching. And yet he was so perturbed in mind and body that he asked himself:

"Is it possible to be afraid in spite of one's self?"

And this doubt, this fearful question, took possession of him. If an irresistible power, stronger than his own will, were to quell his courage, what would happen? He would certainly go to the place appointed; his will would force him that far. But supposing, when there, he were to tremble or faint? And he thought of his social standing, his reputation, his name.

And he suddenly determined to get up and look at himself in the glass. He lighted his candle. When he saw his face reflected in the mirror he scarcely recognized it. He seemed to see before him a man whom he did not know. His eyes looked disproportionately large, and he was very pale.

He remained standing before the mirror. He put out his tongue, as if to examine the state of his health, and all at once the thought flashed into his mind:

"At this time the day after to-morrow I may be dead."

And his heart throbbed painfully.

"At this time the day after to-morrow I may be dead. This person in front of me, this 'I' whom I see in the glass, will perhaps be no more. What! Here I am, I look at myself, I feel myself to be alive—and yet in twenty-four hours I may be lying on that bed, with closed eyes, dead, cold, inanimate."

He turned round, and could see himself distinctly lying on his back on the couch he had just quitted. He had the hollow face and the limp hands of death.

Then he became afraid of his bed, and to avoid seeing it went to his smoking-room. He mechanically took a cigar, lighted it, and began walking back and forth. He was cold; he took a step toward the bell, to wake his valet, but stopped with hand raised toward the bell rope.

"He would see that I am afraid!"

And, instead of ringing, he made a fire himself. His hands quivered nervously as they touched various objects. His head grew dizzy, his thoughts confused, disjointed, painful; a numbness seized his spirit, as if he had been drinking.

And all the time he kept on saying:

"What shall I do? What will become of me?"

His whole body trembled spasmodically; he rose, and, going to the window, drew back the curtains.

The day—a summer day-was breaking. The pink sky cast a glow

on the city, its roofs, and its walls. A flush of light enveloped the awakened world, like a caress from the rising sun, and the glimmer of dawn kindled new hope in the breast of the vicomte. What a fool he was to let himself succumb to fear before anything was decided—before his seconds had interviewed those of Georges Lamil, before he even knew whether he would have to fight or not!

He bathed, dressed, and left the house with a firm step.

He repeated as he went:

"I must be firm—very firm. I must show that I am not afraid."

His seconds, the marquis and the colonel, placed themselves at his disposal, and, having shaken him warmly by the hand, began to discuss details.

"You want a serious duel?" asked the colonel.

"Yes—quite serious," replied the vicomte.

"You insist on pistols?" put in the marquis.

"Yes."

"Do you leave all the other arrangements in our hands?"

With a dry, jerky voice the vicomte answered:

"Twenty paces—at a given signal—the arm to be raised, not lowered—shots to be exchanged until one or other is seriously wounded."

"Excellent conditions," declared the colonel in a satisfied tone. "You are a good shot; all the chances are in your favor."

And they parted. The vicomte returned home to wait for them. His agitation, only temporarily allayed, now increased momentarily. He felt, in arms, legs and chest, a sort of trembling—a continuous vibration; he could not stay still, either sitting or standing. His mouth was parched, and he made every now and then a clicking movement of the tongue, as if to detach it from his palate.

He attempted, to take luncheon, but could not eat. Then it occurred to him to seek courage in drink, and he sent for a decanter of rum, of which he swallowed, one after another, six small glasses.

A burning warmth, followed by a deadening of the mental faculties, ensued. He said to himself:

"I know how to manage. Now it will be all right!"

But at the end of an hour he had emptied the decanter, and his agitation was worse than ever. A mad longing possessed him to throw himself on the ground, to bite, to scream. Night fell.

A ring at the bell so unnerved him that he had not the strength to rise to receive his seconds.

He dared not even to speak to them, wish them good-day, utter a single word, lest his changed voice should betray him.

"All is arranged as you wished," said the colonel. "Your adversary claimed at first the privilege of the offended part; but he yielded almost at once, and accepted your conditions. His seconds are two military men."

"Thank you," said the vicomte.

The marquis added:

"Please excuse us if we do not stay now, for we have a good deal to see to yet. We shall want a reliable doctor, since the duel is not to end until a serious wound has been inflicted; and you know that bullets are not to be trifled with. We must select a spot near some house to which the wounded party can be carried if necessary. In fact, the arrangements will take us another two or three hours at least."

The vicomte articulated for the second time:

"Thank you."

"You're all right?" asked the colonel. "Quite calm?"

"Perfectly calm, thank you."

The two men withdrew.

When he was once more alone he felt as though he should go mad. His servant having lighted the lamps, he sat down at his table to write some letters. When he had traced at the top of a sheet of paper the words: "This is my last will and testament," he started from his seat, feeling himself incapable of connected thought, of decision in regard to anything.

So he was going to fight! He could no longer avoid it. What, then, possessed him? He wished to fight, he was fully determined to fight, and yet, in spite of all his mental effort, in spite of the exertion of all his will power, he felt that he could not even preserve the strength necessary to carry him through the ordeal. He tried to conjure up a picture of the duel, his own attitude, and that of his enemy.

Every now and then his teeth chattered audibly. He thought he would read, and took down Chateauvillard's Rules of Dueling. Then he said:

"Is the other man practiced in the use of the pistol? Is he well known? How can I find out?"

He remembered Baron de Vaux's book on marksmen, and searched it from end to end. Georges Lamil was not mentioned. And yet, if he were not an adept, would he have accepted without demur such a dangerous weapon and such deadly conditions?

He opened a case of Gastinne Renettes which stood on a small table, and took from it a pistol. Next he stood in the correct attitude for firing, and raised his arm. But he was trembling from head to foot, and the weapon shook in his grasp.

Then he said to himself:

"It is impossible. I cannot fight like this."

He looked at the little black, death-spitting hole at the end of the pistol; he thought of dishonor, of the whispers at the clubs, the smiles in his friends' drawing-rooms, the contempt of women, the veiled sneers of the newspapers, the insults that would be hurled at him by cowards.

He still looked at the weapon, and raising the hammer, saw the glitter of the priming below it. The pistol had been left loaded by some chance, some oversight. And the discovery rejoiced him, he knew not why.

If he did not maintain, in presence of his opponent, the steadfast bearing which was so necessary to his honor, he would be ruined forever. He would be branded, stigmatized as a coward, hounded out of society! And he felt, he knew, that he could not maintain that calm, unmoved demeanor. And yet he was brave, since the thought that followed was not even rounded to a finish in his mind; but, opening his mouth wide, he suddenly plunged the barrel of the pistol as far back as his throat, and pressed the trigger.

When the valet, alarmed at the report, rushed into the room he found his master lying dead upon his back. A spurt of blood had splashed the white paper on the table, and had made a great crimson stain beneath the words:

"This is my last will and testament."

OLD MONGILET

*J*n the office old Mongilet was considered a type. He was a good old employee, who had never been outside Paris but once in his life.

It was the end of July, and each of us, every Sunday, went to roll in the grass, or soak in the water in the country near by. Asnieres, Argenteuil, Chatou, Borgival, Maisons, Poissy, had their habitues and their ardent admirers. We argued about the merits and advantages of all these places, celebrated and delightful to all Parsian employees.

Daddy Mongilet declared:

"You are like a lot of sheep! It must be pretty, this country you talk of!"

"Well, how about you, Mongilet? Don't you ever go on an excursion?"

"Yes, indeed. I go in an omnibus. When I have had a good luncheon, without any hurry, at the wine shop down there, I look up my route with a plan of Paris, and the time table of the lines and connections. And then I climb up on the box, open my umbrella and off we go. Oh, I see lots of things, more than you, I bet! I change my surroundings. It is as though I were taking a journey across the world, the people are so different in one street and another. I know my Paris better than anyone. And then, there is nothing more amusing than the entresols. You would not believe what one sees in there at a glance. One guesses at domestic scenes simply at sight of the face of a man who is roaring; one is amused on passing by a barber's shop, to see the barber leave his customer whose face is covered with lather to look out in the street. One exchanges heartfelt glances with the milliners just for fun, as one has no time to alight. Ah, how many things one sees!

"It is the drama, the real, the true, the drama of nature, seen as the horses trot by. Heavens! I would not give my excursions in the omnibus for all your stupid excursions in the woods."

"Come and try it, Mongilet, come to the country once just to see."

"I was there once," he replied, "twenty years ago, and you will never catch me there again."

"Tell us about it, Mongilet."

"If you wish to hear it. This is how it was:

"You knew Boivin, the old editorial clerk, whom we called Boileau?"

"Yes, perfectly."

"He was my office chum. The rascal had a house at Colombes and always invited me to spend Sunday with him. He would say:

"'Come along, Maculotte [he called me Maculotte for fun]. You will see what a nice excursion we will take.'

"I let myself be entrapped like an animal, and set out, one morning by the 8 o'clock train. I arrived at a kind of town, a country town where there is nothing to see, and I at length found my way to an old wooden door with an iron bell, at the end of an alley between two walls.

"I rang, and waited a long time, and at last the door was opened. What was it that opened it? I could not tell at the first glance. A woman or an ape? The creature was old, ugly, covered with old clothes that looked dirty and wicked. It had chicken's feathers in its hair and looked as though it would devour me.

"'What do you want?' she said.

"'Mr. Boivin.'

"'What do you want of him, of Mr. Boivin?'

"I felt ill at ease on being questioned by this fury. I stammered: 'Why-he expects me.'

"'Ah, it is you who have come to luncheon?'

"'Yes,' I stammered, trembling.

"Then, turning toward the house, she cried in an angry tone:

"'Boivin, here is your man!'

"It was my friend's wife. Little Boivin appeared immediately on the threshold of a sort of barrack of plaster covered with zinc, that looked like a foot stove. He wore white duck trousers covered with stains and a dirty Panama hat.

"After shaking my hands warmly, he took me into what he called his garden. It was at the end of another alleyway enclosed by high walls and was a little square the size of a pocket handkerchief, surrounded by houses that were so high that the sun, could reach it only two or three hours in the day. Pansies, pinks, wallflowers and a few rose bushes were languishing in this well without air, and hot as an oven from the refraction of heat from the roofs.

"'I have no trees,' said Boivin, 'but the neighbors' walls take their place. I have as much shade as in a wood.'

"Then he took hold of a button of my coat and said in a low tone:

"'You can do me a service. You saw the wife. She is not agreeable, eh? To-day, as I had invited you, she gave me clean clothes; but if I spot them all is lost. I counted on you to water my plants.'

"I agreed. I took off my coat, rolled up my sleeves, and began to work the handle of a kind of pump that wheezed, puffed and rattled like a consumptive as it emitted a thread of water like a Wallace drinking fountain. It took me ten minutes to water it and I was in a bath of perspiration. Boivin directed me:

"'Here—this plant—a little more; enough—now this one.'

"The watering pot leaked and my feet got more water than the flowers. The bottoms of my trousers were soaking and covered with mud. And twenty times running I kept it up, soaking my feet afresh each time, and perspiring anew as I worked the handle of the pump. And when I was tired out and wanted to stop, Boivin, in a tone of entreaty, said as he put his hand on my arm:

"Just one more watering pot full—just one, and that will be all.'

"To thank me he gave me a rose, a big rose, but hardly had it touched my button-hole than it fell to pieces, leaving only a hard little green knot as a decoration. I was surprised, but said nothing.

"Mme. Boivin's voice was heard in the distance:

"'Are you ever coming? When you know that luncheon is ready!'

"We went toward the foot stove. If the garden was in the shade, the house, on the other hand, was in the blazing sun, and the sweating room in the Turkish bath is not as hot as was my friend's dining room.

"Three plates at the side of which were some half-washed forks, were placed on a table of yellow wood in the middle of which stood an earthenware dish containing boiled beef and potatoes. We began to eat.

"A large water bottle full of water lightly colored with wine attracted my attention. Boivin, embarrassed, said to his wife:

"'See here, my dear, just on a special occasion, are you not going to give us some plain wine?'

"She looked at him furiously.

"'So that you may both get tipsy, is that it, and stay here gabbing all day? A fig for your special occasion!'

"He said no more. After the stew she brought in another dish of potatoes cooked with bacon. When this dish was finished, still in silence, she announced:

"'That is all! Now get out!'

"Boivin looked at her in astonishment.

"'But the pigeon—the pigeon you plucked this morning?'

"She put her hands on her hips:

"'Perhaps you have not had enough? Because you bring people here is no reason why we should devour all that there is in the house. What is there for me to eat this evening?'

"We rose. Solvin whispered

"'Wait for me a second, and we will skip.'

"He went into the kitchen where his wife had gone, and I overheard him say:

"'Give me twenty sous, my dear.'

"'What do you want with twenty sons?'

"'Why, one does not know what may happen. It is always better to have some money.'

"She yelled so that I should hear:

"'No, I will not give it to you! As the man has had luncheon here, the least he can do is to pay your expenses for the day.'

"Boivin came back to fetch me. As I wished to be polite I bowed to the mistress of the house, stammering:

"'Madame—many thanks—kind welcome.'

"'That's all right,' she replied. 'But do not bring him back drunk, for you will have to answer to me, you know!'

"We set out. We had to cross a perfectly bare plain under the burning sun. I attempted to gather a flower along the road and gave a cry of pain. It had hurt my hand frightfully. They call these plants nettles. And, everywhere, there was a smell of manure, enough to turn your stomach.

"Boivin said, 'Have a little patience and we will reach the river bank.'

"We reached the river. Here there was an odor of mud and dirty water, and the sun blazed down on the water so that it burned my eyes. I begged Boivin to go under cover somewhere. He took me into a kind of shanty filled with men, a river boatmen's tavern.

"He said:

"'This does not look very grand, but it is very comfortable.'

"I was hungry. I ordered an omelet. But to and behold, at the second glass of wine, that beggar, Boivin, lost his head, and I understand why his wife gave him water diluted.

"He got up, declaimed, wanted to show his strength, interfered in a quarrel between two drunken men who were fighting, and, but for the landlord, who came to the rescue, we should both have been killed.

"I dragged him away, holding him up until we reached the first bush where I deposited him. I lay down beside him and, it seems, I fell asleep. We must certainly have slept a long time, for it was dark when I awoke. Boivin was snoring at my side. I shook him; he rose but he was still drunk, though a little less so.

"We set out through the darkness across the plain. Boivin said he knew the way. He made me turn to the left, then to the right, then to the left. We could see neither sky nor earth, and found ourselves lost in the midst of a kind of forest of wooden stakes, that came as high as our noses. It was a vineyard and these were the supports. There was not a single light on the horizon. We wandered about in this vineyard for about an hour or two, hesitating, reaching out our arms without finding any limit, for we kept retracing our steps.

"At length Boivin fell against a stake that tore his cheek and he remained in a sitting posture on the ground, uttering with all his might long and resounding hallos, while I screamed 'Help! Help!' as loud as I could, lighting candle-matches to show the way to our rescuers, and also to keep up my courage.

"At last a belated peasant heard us and put us on our right road. I took Boivin to his home, but as I was leaving him on the threshold of his garden, the door opened suddenly and his wife appeared, a candle in her hand. She frightened me horribly.

"As soon as she saw her husband, whom she must have been waiting for since dark, she screamed, as she darted toward me:

"'Ah, scoundrel, I knew you would bring him back drunk!'

"My, how I made my escape, running all the way to the station, and as I thought the fury was pursuing me I shut myself in an inner room as the train was not due for half an hour.

"That is why I never married, and why I never go out of Paris."

MOONLIGHT

Madame Julie Roubere was expecting her elder sister, Madame Henriette Letore, who had just returned from a trip to Switzerland.

The Letore household had left nearly five weeks before. Madame Henriette had allowed her husband to return alone to their estate in Calvados, where some business required his attention, and had come to spend a few days in Paris with her sister. Night came on. In the quiet parlor Madame Roubere was reading in the twilight in an absent-minded way, raising her, eyes whenever she heard a sound.

At last, she heard a ring at the door, and her sister appeared, wrapped in a travelling cloak. And without any formal greeting, they clasped each other in an affectionate embrace, only desisting for a moment to give each other another hug. Then they talked about their health, about their respective families, and a thousand other things, gossiping, jerking out hurried, broken sentences as they followed each other about, while Madame Henriette was removing her hat and veil.

It was now quite dark. Madame Roubere rang for a lamp, and as soon as it was brought in, she scanned her sister's face, and was on the point of embracing her once more. But she held back, scared and astonished at the other's appearance.

On her temples Madame Letore had two large locks of white hair. All the rest of her hair was of a glossy, raven-black hue; but there alone, at each side of her head, ran, as it were, two silvery streams which were immediately lost in the black mass surrounding them. She was, nevertheless, only twenty-four years old, and this change had come on suddenly since her departure for Switzerland.

Without moving, Madame Roubere gazed at her in amazement, tears rising to her eyes, as she thought that some mysterious and terrible calamity must have befallen her sister. She asked:

"What is the matter with you, Henriette?"

Smiling with a sad face, the smile of one who is heartsick, the other replied:

"Why, nothing, I assure you. Were you noticing my white hair?"

But Madame Roubere impetuously seized her by the shoulders, and with a searching glance at her, repeated:

"What is the matter with you? Tell me what is the matter with you. And if you tell me a falsehood, I'll soon find it out."

They remained face to face, and Madame Henriette, who looked as if she were about to faint, had two pearly tears in the corners of her drooping eyes.

Her sister continued:

"What has happened to you? What is the matter with you? Answer me!"

Then, in a subdued voice, the other murmured:

"I have—I have a lover."

And, hiding her forehead on the shoulder of her younger sister, she sobbed.

Then, when she had grown a little calmer, when the heaving of her breast had subsided, she commenced to unbosom herself, as if to cast forth this secret from herself, to empty this sorrow of hers into a sympathetic heart.

Thereupon, holding each other's hands tightly clasped, the two women went over to a sofa in a dark corner of the room, into which they sank, and the younger sister, passing her arm over the elder one's neck, and drawing her close to her heart, listened.

"Oh! I know that there was no excuse for me; I do not understand myself, and since that day I feel as if I were mad. Be careful, my child, about yourself—be careful! If you only knew how weak we are, how quickly we yield, and fall. It takes so little, so little, so little, a moment of tenderness, one of those sudden fits of melancholy which come over you, one of those longings to open your arms, to love, to cherish something, which we all have at certain moments.

"You know my husband, and you know how fond I am of him; but he is mature and sensible, and cannot even comprehend the tender vibrations of a woman's heart. He is always the same, always good, always smiling, always kind, always perfect. Oh! how I sometimes have wished that he would clasp me roughly in his arms, that he would embrace me with those slow, sweet kisses which make two beings intermingle, which are like mute confidences! How I have wished that he were foolish, even weak, so that he should have need of me, of my caresses, of my tears!

"This all seems very silly; but we women are made like that. How can we help it?

"And yet the thought of deceiving him never entered my mind.

Now it has happened, without love, without reason, without anything, simply because the moon shone one night on the Lake of Lucerne.

"During the month when we were travelling together, my husband, with his calm indifference, paralyzed my enthusiasm, extinguished my poetic ardor. When we were descending the mountain paths at sunrise, when as the four horses galloped along with the diligence, we saw, in the transparent morning haze, valleys, woods, streams, and villages, I clasped my hands with delight, and said to him: 'How beautiful it is, dear! Give me a kiss! Kiss me now!' He only answered, with a smile of chilling kindliness: 'There is no reason why we should kiss each other because you like the landscape.'

"And his words froze me to the heart. It seems to me that when people love each other, they ought to feel more moved by love than ever, in the presence of beautiful scenes.

"In fact, I was brimming over with poetry which he kept me from expressing. I was almost like a boiler filled with steam and hermetically sealed.

"One evening (we had for four days been staying in a hotel at Fluelen) Robert, having one of his sick headaches, went to bed immediately after dinner, and I went to take a walk all alone along the edge of the lake.

"It was a night such as one reads of in fairy tales. The full moon showed itself in the middle of the sky; the tall mountains, with their snowy crests, seemed to wear silver crowns; the waters of the lake glittered with tiny shining ripples. The air was mild, with that kind of penetrating warmth which enervates us till we are ready to faint, to be deeply affected without any apparent cause. But how sensitive, how vibrating the heart is at such moments! how quickly it beats, and how intense is its emotion!

"I sat down on the grass, and gazed at that vast, melancholy, and fascinating lake, and a strange feeling arose in me; I was seized with an insatiable need of love, a revolt against the gloomy dullness of my life. What! would it never be my fate to wander, arm in arm, with a man I loved, along a moon-kissed bank like this? Was I never to feel on my lips those kisses so deep, delicious, and intoxicating which lovers exchange on nights that seem to have been made by God for tenderness? Was I never to know ardent, feverish love in the moonlit shadows of a summer's night?

"And I burst out weeping like a crazy woman. I heard something stirring behind me. A man stood there, gazing at me. When I turned my head round, he recognized me, and, advancing, said:

49

"'You are weeping, madame?'

"It was a young barrister who was travelling with his mother, and whom we had often met. His eyes had frequently followed me.

"I was so confused that I did not know what answer to give or what to think of the situation. I told him I felt ill.

"He walked on by my side in a natural and respectful manner, and began talking to me about what we had seen during our trip. All that I had felt he translated into words; everything that made me thrill he understood perfectly, better than I did myself. And all of a sudden he repeated some verses of Alfred de Musset. I felt myself choking, seized with indescribable emotion. It seemed to me that the mountains themselves, the lake, the moonlight, were singing to me about things ineffably sweet.

"And it happened, I don't know how, I don't know why, in a sort of hallucination.

"As for him, I did not see him again till the morning of his departure.

"He gave me his card!"

And, sinking into her sister's arms, Madame Letore broke into groans —almost into shrieks.

Then, Madame Roubere, with a self-contained and serious air, said very gently:

"You see, sister, very often it is not a man that we love, but love itself. And your real lover that night was the moonlight."

THE FIRST SNOWFALL

The long promenade of La Croisette winds in a curve along the edge of the blue water. Yonder, to the right, Esterel juts out into the sea in the distance, obstructing the view and shutting out the horizon with its pretty southern outline of pointed summits, numerous and fantastic.

To the left, the isles of Sainte Marguerite and Saint Honorat, almost level with the water, display their surface, covered with pine trees.

And all along the great gulf, all along the tall mountains that encircle Cannes, the white villa residences seem to be sleeping in the sunlight. You can see them from a distance, the white houses, scattered from the top to the bottom of the mountains, dotting the dark greenery with specks like snow.

Those near the water have gates opening on the wide promenade which is washed by the quiet waves. The air is soft and balmy. It is one of those warm winter days when there is scarcely a breath of cool air. Above the walls of the gardens may be seen orange trees and lemon trees full of golden fruit. Ladies are walking slowly across the sand of the avenue, followed by children rolling hoops, or chatting with gentlemen.

A young woman has just passed out through the door of her coquettish little house facing La Croisette. She stops for a moment to gaze at the promenaders, smiles, and with an exhausted air makes her way toward an empty bench facing the sea. Fatigued after having gone twenty paces, she sits down out of breath. Her pale face seems that of a dead woman. She coughs, and raises to her lips her transparent fingers as if to stop those paroxysms that exhaust her.

She gazes at the sky full of sunshine and swallows, at the zigzag summits of the Esterel over yonder, and at the sea, the blue, calm, beautiful sea, close beside her.

She smiles again, and murmurs:

"Oh! how happy I am!"

She knows, however, that she is going to die, that she will never see the springtime, that in a year, along the same promenade, these same people who pass before her now will come again to breathe the warm air of this charming spot, with their children a little bigger, with their hearts all filled with hopes, with tenderness, with happiness, while at the bottom of an oak coffin, the poor flesh which is still left to her to-day will have decomposed, leaving only her bones lying in the silk robe which she has selected for a shroud.

She will be no more. Everything in life will go on as before for others. For her, life will be over, over forever. She will be no more. She smiles, and inhales as well as she can, with her diseased lungs, the perfumed air of the gardens.

And she sinks into a reverie.

She recalls the past. She had been married, four years ago, to a Norman gentleman. He was a strong young man, bearded, healthy-looking, with wide shoulders, narrow mind, and joyous disposition.

They had been united through financial motives which she knew nothing about. She would willingly have said No. She said Yes, with a movement of the head, in order not to thwart her father and mother. She was a Parisian, gay, and full of the joy of living.

Her husband brought her home to his Norman chateau. It was a huge stone building surrounded by tall trees of great age. A high clump of pine trees shut out the view in front. On the right, an opening in the trees presented a view of the plain, which stretched out in an unbroken level as far as the distant, farmsteads. A crossroad passed before the gate and led to the high road three kilometres away.

Oh! she recalls everything, her arrival, her first day in her new abode, and her isolated life afterward.

When she stepped out of the carriage, she glanced at the old building, and laughingly exclaimed:

"It does not look cheerful!"

Her husband began to laugh in his turn, and replied:

"Pooh! we get used to it! You'll see. I never feel bored in it, for my part."

That day they passed their time in embracing each other, and she did not find it too long. This lasted fully a month. The days passed one after the other in insignificant yet absorbing occupations. She learned the value and the importance of the little things of life. She knew that people can interest themselves in the price of eggs, which cost a few centimes more or less according to the seasons.

It was summer. She went to the fields to see the men harvesting. The brightness of the sunshine found an echo in her heart.

The autumn came. Her husband went out shooting. He started in the morning with his two dogs Medor and Mirza. She remained alone, without grieving, moreover, at Henry's absence. She was very fond of him, but she did not miss him. When he returned home, her affection was especially bestowed on the dogs. She took care of them every evening with a mother's tenderness, caressed them incessantly, gave them a thousand charming little names which she had no idea of applying to her husband.

He invariably told her all about his sport. He described the places where he found partridges, expressed his astonishment at not having caught any hares in Joseph Ledentu's clever, or else appeared indignant at the conduct of M. Lechapelier, of Havre, who always went along the edge of his property to shoot the game that he, Henry de Parville, had started.

She replied: "Yes, indeed! it is not right," thinking of something else all the while.

The winter came, the Norman winter, cold and rainy. The endless floods of rain came down on the slates of the great gabled roof, rising like a knife blade toward the sky. The roads seemed like rivers of mud, the country a plain of mud, and no sound could be heard save that of water falling; no movement could be seen save the whirling flight of crows that settled down like a cloud on a field and then hurried off again.

About four o'clock, the army of dark, flying creatures came and perched in the tall beeches at the left of the chateau, emitting deafening cries. During nearly an hour, they flew from tree top to tree top, seemed to be fighting, croaked, and made a black disturbance in the gray branches. She gazed at them each evening with a weight at her heart, so deeply was she impressed by the lugubrious melancholy of the darkness falling on the deserted country.

Then she rang for the lamp, and drew near the fire. She burned heaps of wood without succeeding in warming the spacious apartments reeking with humidity. She was cold all day long, everywhere, in the drawing-room, at meals, in her own apartment. It seemed to her she was cold to the marrow of her bones. Her husband only came in to dinner; he was always out shooting, or else he was superintending sowing the seed, tilling the soil, and all the work of the country.

He would come back jovial, and covered with mud, rubbing his hands as he exclaimed:

"What wretched weather!"

Or else:

"A fire looks comfortable!"

Or sometimes:

"Well, how are you to-day? Are you in good spirits?"

He was happy, in good health, without desires, thinking of nothing save this simple, healthy, and quiet life.

About December, when the snow had come, she suffered so much from the icy-cold air of the chateau which seemed to have become chilled in passing through the centuries just as human beings become chilled with years, that she asked her husband one evening:

"Look here, Henry! You ought to have a furnace put into the house; it would dry the walls. I assure you that I cannot keep warm from morning till night."

At first he was stunned at this extravagant idea of introducing a furnace into his manor-house. It would have seemed more natural to him to have his dogs fed out of silver dishes. He gave a tremendous laugh from the bottom of his chest as he exclaimed:

"A furnace here! A furnace here! Ha! ha! ha! what a good joke!"

She persisted:

"I assure you, dear, I feel frozen; you don't feel it because you are always moving about; but all the same, I feel frozen."

He replied, still laughing:

"Pooh! you'll get used to it, and besides it is excellent for the health. You will only be all the better for it. We are not Parisians, damn it! to live in hot-houses. And, besides, the spring is quite near."

About the beginning of January, a great misfortune befell her. Her father and mother died in a carriage accident. She came to Paris for the funeral. And her sorrow took entire possession of her mind for about six months.

The mildness of the beautiful summer days finally roused her, and she lived along in a state of sad languor until autumn.

When the cold weather returned, she was brought face to face, for the first time, with the gloomy future. What was she to do? Nothing. What was going to happen to her henceforth? Nothing. What expectation, what hope, could revive her heart? None. A doctor who was consulted declared that she would never have children.

Sharper, more penetrating still than the year before, the cold made her suffer continually.

She stretched out her shivering hands to the big flames. The glaring fire burned her face; but icy whiffs seemed to glide down her back and to penetrate between her skin and her underclothing. And she shivered from head to foot. Innumerable draughts of air appeared to have taken up their abode in the apartment, living, crafty currents of air as cruel as enemies. She encountered them at every moment; they blew on her incessantly their perfidious and frozen hatred, now on her face, now on her hands, and now on her back.

Once more she spoke of a furnace; but her husband listened to her request as if she were asking for the moon. The introduction of such an apparatus at Parville appeared to him as impossible as the discovery of the Philosopher's Stone.

Having been at Rouen on business one day, he brought back to his wife a dainty foot warmer made of copper, which he laughingly called a "portable furnace"; and he considered that this would prevent her henceforth from ever being cold.

Toward the end of December she understood that she could not always live like this, and she said timidly one evening at dinner:

"Listen, dear! Are we not going to spend a week or two in Paris before spring:"

He was stupefied.

"In Paris? In Paris? But what are we to do there? Ah! no by Jove! We are better off here. What odd ideas come into your head sometimes."

She faltered:

"It might distract us a little."

He did not understand.

"What is it you want to distract you? Theatres, evening parties, dinners in town? You knew, however, when you came here, that you ought not to expect any distractions of this kind!"

She saw a reproach in these words, and in the tone in which they were uttered. She relapsed into silence. She was timid and gentle, without resisting power and without strength of will.

In January the cold weather returned with violence. Then the snow covered the earth.

One evening, as she watched the great black cloud of crows dispersing among the trees, she began to weep, in spite of herself.

Her husband came in. He asked in great surprise:

"What is the matter with you?"

He was happy, quite happy, never having dreamed of another life or other pleasures. He had been born and had grown up in this melancholy district. He felt contented in his own house, at ease in body and mind.

He did not understand that one might desire incidents, have a longing for changing pleasures; he did not understand that it does not seem natural to certain beings to remain in the same place during the four seasons; he seemed not to know that spring, summer, autumn, and winter have, for multitudes of persons, fresh amusements in new places.

She could say nothing in reply, and she quickly dried her eyes. At last she murmured in a despairing tone:

"I am—I—I am a little sad—I am a little bored."

But she was terrified at having even said so much, and added very quickly:

"And, besides—I am—I am a little cold."

This last plea made him angry.

"Ah! yes, still your idea of the furnace. But look here, deuce take it! you have not had one cold since you came here."

Night came on. She went up to her room, for she had insisted on having a separate apartment. She went to bed. Even in bed she felt cold. She thought:

"It will be always like this, always, until I die."

And she thought of her husband. How could he have said:

"You—have not had one cold since you came here"?

She would have to be ill, to cough before he could understand what she suffered!

And she was filled with indignation, the angry indignation of a weak, timid being.

She must cough. Then, perhaps, he would take pity on her. Well, she would cough; he should hear her coughing; the doctor should be called in; he should see, her husband, he should see.

She got out of bed, her legs and her feet bare, and a childish idea made her smile:

"I want a furnace, and I must have it. I shall cough so much that he'll have to put one in the house."

And she sat down in a chair in her nightdress. She waited an hour, two hours. She shivered, but she did not catch cold. Then she resolved on a bold expedient.

She noiselessly left her room, descended the stairs, and opened the gate into the garden.

The earth, covered with snows seemed dead. She abruptly thrust forward her bare foot, and plunged it into the icy, fleecy snow. A sensation of cold, painful as a wound, mounted to her heart. However, she stretched out the other leg, and began to descend the steps slowly.

Then she advanced through the grass saying to herself:

"I'll go as far as the pine trees."

She walked with quick steps, out of breath, gasping every time she plunged her foot into the snow.

She touched the first pine tree with her hand, as if to assure herself that she had carried out her plan to the end; then she went back into the house. She thought two or three times that she was going to fall, so numbed and weak did she feel. Before going in, however, she sat down in that icy fleece, and even took up several handfuls to rub on her chest.

Then she went in and got into bed. It seemed to her at the end of an hour that she had a swarm of ants in her throat, and that other ants were running all over her limbs. She slept, however.

Next day she was coughing and could not get up.

She had inflammation of the lungs. She became delirious, and in her delirium she asked for a furnace. The doctor insisted on having one put in. Henry yielded, but with visible annoyance.

She was incurable. Her lungs were seriously affected, and those about her feared for her life.

"If she remains here, she will not last until the winter," said the doctor.

She was sent south. She came to Cannes, made the acquaintance of the sun, loved the sea, and breathed the perfume of orange blossoms.

Then, in the spring, she returned north.

But she now lived with the fear of being cured, with the fear of the long winters of Normandy; and as soon as she was better she opened her window by night and recalled the sweet shores of the Mediterranean.

And now she is going to die. She knows it and she is happy.

She unfolds a newspaper which she has not already opened, and reads this heading:

"The first snow in Paris."

She shivers and then smiles. She looks across at the Esterel, which is becoming rosy in the rays of the setting sun. She looks at the vast blue sky, so blue, so very blue, and the vast blue sea, so very blue also, and she rises from her seat.

And then she returned to the house with slow steps, only stopping to cough, for she had remained out too long and she was cold, a little cold.

She finds a letter from her husband. She opens it, still smiling, and she reads:

"MY DEAR LOVE: I hope you are well, and that you do not regret too much our beautiful country. For some days last we have had a good

frost, which presages snow. For my part, I adore this weather, and

you may believe that I do not light your damned furnace."

She ceases reading, quite happy at the thought that she had her furnace put in. Her right hand, which holds the letter, falls slowly on her lap, while she raises her left hand to her mouth, as if to calm the obstinate cough which is racking her chest.

SUNDAYS OF A BOURGEOIS

PREPARATIONS FOR THE EXCURSION

M. Patissot, born in Paris, after having failed in his examinations at the College Henri IV., like many others, had entered the government service through the influence of one of his aunts, who kept a tobacco store where the head of one of the departments bought his provisions.

He advanced very slowly, and would, perhaps, have died a fourth-class clerk without the aid of a kindly Providence, which sometimes watches over our destiny. He is today fifty-two years old, and it is only at this age that he is beginning to explore, as a tourist, all that part of France which lies between the fortifications and the provinces.

The story of his advance might be useful to many employees, just as the tale of his excursions may be of value to many Parisians who will take them as a model for their own outings, and will thus, through his example, avoid certain mishaps which occurred to him.

In 1854 he only enjoyed a salary of 1,800 francs. Through a peculiar trait of his character he was unpopular with all his superiors, who let him languish in the eternal and hopeless expectation of the clerk's ideal, an increase of salary. Nevertheless he worked; but he did not know how to make himself appreciated. He had too much self-respect, he claimed. His self-respect consisted in never bowing to his superiors in a low and servile manner, as did, according to him, certain of his colleagues, whom he would not mention. He added that his frankness embarrassed many people, for, like all the rest, he protested against injustice and the favoritism shown to persons entirely foreign to the bureaucracy. But his indignant voice never passed beyond the little cage where he worked.

First as a government clerk, then as a Frenchman and finally as a man who believed in order he would adhere to whatever government was established, having an unbounded reverence for authority, except for that of his chiefs.

Each time that he got the chance he would place himself where he could see the emperor pass, in order to have the honor of taking his hat off to him; and he would go away puffed up with pride at having bowed to the head of the state.

From his habit of observing the sovereign he did as many others do; he imitated the way he trimmed his beard or arranged his hair, the cut of his clothes, his walk, his mannerisms. Indeed, how many men in each country seemed to be the living images of the head of the government! Perhaps he vaguely resembled Napoleon III., but his hair was black; therefore he dyed it, and then the likeness was complete; and when he met another gentleman in the street also imitating the imperial countenance he was jealous and looked at him disdainfully. This need of imitation soon became his hobby, and, having heard an usher at the Tuilleries imitate the voice of the emperor, he also acquired the same intonations and studied slowness.

He thus became so much like his model that they might easily have been mistaken for each other, and certain high dignitaries were heard to remark that they found it unseemly and even vulgar; the matter was mentioned to the prime minister, who ordered that the employee should appear before him. But at the sight of him he began to laugh and repeated two or three times: "That's funny, really funny!" This was repeated, and the following day Patissot's immediate superior recommended that his subordinate receive an increase of salary of three hundred francs. He received it immediately.

From that time on his promotions came regularly, thanks to his ape-like faculty of imitation. The presentiment that some high honor might come to him some day caused his chiefs to speak to him with deference.

When the Republic was proclaimed it was a disaster for him. He felt lost, done for, and, losing his head, he stopped dyeing his hair, shaved his face clean and had his hair cut short, thus acquiring a paternal and benevolent expression which could not compromise him in any way.

Then his chiefs took revenge for the long time during which he had imposed upon them, and, having all turned Republican through an instinct of self preservation, they cut down his salary and delayed his promotion. He, too, changed his opinions. But the Republic not being a palpable and living person whom one can resemble, and the presidents succeeding each other with rapidity, he found himself plunged in the greatest embarrassment, in terrible distress, and, after an unsuccessful imitation of his last ideal, M. Thiers, he felt a check put on all his attempts at imitation. He needed a new manifestation of his personality. He searched for a long time; then, one morning, he arrived at the office wearing a new hat which had on the side a small red, white and blue rosette. His colleagues were astounded; they laughed all that day, the next day, all the week, all the month. But the seriousness of his demeanor at last disconcerted them, and once more his superiors became anxious. What mystery could be hidden under this sign? Was it a simple manifestation of patriotism, or an affirmation of his allegiance to the Republic, or perhaps the badge of some powerful association? But to wear it so persistently he must surely have some powerful and hidden protection. It would be well to be on one's guard, especially as he received all pleasantries with unruffled calmness. After that he was treated with respect, and his sham courage saved him; he was appointed head clerk on the first of January, 1880. His whole life had been spent indoors. He hated noise and bustle, and because of this love of rest and quiet he had remained a bachelor. He spent his Sundays reading tales of adventure and ruling guide lines which he afterward offered to his colleagues. In his whole existence he had only taken three vacations of a week each, when he was changing his quarters. But sometimes, on a holiday, he would leave by an excursion train for Dieppe or Havre in order to elevate his mind by the inspiring sight of the sea.

He was full of that common sense which borders on stupidity. For a long time he had been living quietly, with economy, temperate through prudence, chaste by temperament, when suddenly he was assailed by a terrible apprehension. One evening in the street he suddenly felt an attack of dizziness which made him fear a stroke of apoplexy. He hastened to a physician and for five francs obtained the following prescription:

M. X-, fifty-five years old, bachelor, clerk. Full-blooded, danger of apoplexy. Cold-water applications, moderate nourishment, plenty of exercise.   MONTELLIER, M.D.

Patissot was greatly distressed, and for a whole month, in his office, he kept a wet towel wrapped around his head like a turban while the water continually dripped on his work, which he would have to do over again. Every once in a while he would read the prescription over, probably in the hope of finding some hidden meaning, of penetrating into the secret thought of the physician, and also of discovering some forms of exercise which, might perhaps make him immune from apoplexy.

Then he consulted his friends, showing them the fateful paper. One advised boxing. He immediately hunted up an instructor, and, on the first day, he received a punch in the nose which immediately took away all his ambition in this direction. Single-stick made him gasp for breath, and he grew so stiff from fencing that for two days and two nights he could not get sleep. Then a bright idea struck him. It was to walk, every Sunday, to some suburb of Paris and even to certain places in the capital which he did not know.

For a whole week his mind was occupied with thoughts of the equipment which you need for these excursions; and on Sunday, the 30th of May, he began his preparations. After reading all the extraordinary advertisements which poor, blind and halt beggars distribute on the street corners, he began to visit the stores with the intention of looking about him only and of buying later on. First of all, he visited a so-called American shoe store, where heavy travelling shoes were shown him. The clerk brought out a kind of ironclad contrivance, studded with spikes like a harrow, which he claimed to be made from Rocky Mountain bison skin. He was so carried away with them that he would willingly have bought two pair, but one was sufficient. He carried them away under his arm, which soon became numb from the weight. He next invested in a pair of corduroy trousers, such as carpenters wear, and a pair of oiled canvas leggings. Then he needed a knapsack for his provisions, a telescope so as to recognize villages perched on the slope of distant hills, and finally, a government survey map to enable him to find his way about without asking the peasants toiling in the fields. Lastly, in order more comfortably to stand the heat, he decided to purchase a light alpaca jacket offered by the famous firm of Raminau, according to their advertisement, for the modest sum of six francs and fifty centimes. He went to this store and was welcomed by a distinguished-looking young man with a marvellous head of hair, nails as pink as those of a lady and a pleasant smile. He showed him the garment. It did not correspond with the glowing style of the advertisement. Then Patissot hesitatingly asked, "Well, monsieur, will it wear well?" The young man turned his eyes away in well-feigned embarrassment, like an honest man who does not wish to deceive a customer, and, lowering his eyes, he said in a hesitating manner: "Dear me, monsieur, you understand that for six francs fifty we cannot turn out an article like this for instance." And he showed him a much finer jacket than the first one. Patissot examined it and asked the price. "Twelve francs fifty." It was very tempting, but before deciding, he once more questioned the big young man, who was observing him attentively. "And—is that good? Do you guarantee it?" "Oh! certainly, monsieur, it is quite good! But, of course, you must not get it wet! Yes, it's really quite good, but you understand that there are goods and goods. It's excellent for the price. Twelve francs fifty, just think. Why, that's nothing at all. Naturally a twenty-five-franc coat is much better. For twenty-five francs you get a superior quality, as strong as linen, and which wears even better. If it gets wet a little ironing will fix it right up. The color never fades, and it does not turn red in the sunlight. It is the warmest and lightest material out." He unfolded his wares, holding them up, shaking them, crumpling and stretching them in order to show the excellent quality of the cloth. He talked on convincingly, dispelling all hesitation by words and gesture. Patissot was convinced; he bought the coat. The pleasant salesman, still talking, tied up the bundle and continued praising the value of the purchase. When it was paid for he was suddenly silent. He bowed with a superior air, and, holding the door open, he watched his customer disappear, both arms filled with bundles and vainly trying to reach his hat to bow.

M. Patissot returned home and carefully studied the map. He wished to try on his shoes, which were more like skates than shoes, owing to the spikes. He slipped and fell, promising himself to be more careful in the future. Then he spread out all his purchases on a chair and looked at them for a long time. He went to sleep with this thought: "Isn't it strange that I didn't think before of taking an excursion to the country?"

During the whole week Patissot worked without ambition. He was dreaming of the outing which he had planned for the following Sunday, and he was seized by a sudden longing for the country, a desire of growing tender over nature, this thirst for rustic scenes which overwhelms the Parisians in spring time.

Only one person gave him any attention; it was a silent old copying clerk named Boivin, nicknamed Boileau. He himself lived in the country and had a little garden which he cultivated carefully; his needs were small, and he was perfectly happy, so they said. Patissot was now able to understand his tastes and the similarity of their ideals made them immediately fast friends. Old man Boivin said to him:

"Do I like fishing, monsieur? Why, it's the delight of my life!"

Then Patissot questioned him with deep interest. Boivin named all the fish who frolicked under this dirty water—and Patissot thought he could see them. Boivin told about the different hooks, baits, spots and times suitable for each kind. And Patissot felt himself more like a fisherman than Boivin himself. They decided that the following Sunday they would meet for the opening of the season for the edification of Patissot, who was delighted to have found such an experienced instructor.

FISHING EXCURSION

The day before the one when he was, for the first time in his life, to throw a hook into a river, Monsieur Patissot bought, for eighty centimes, "How to Become a Perfect Fisherman." In this work he learned many useful things, but he was especially impressed by the style, and he retained the following passage:

"In a word, if you wish, without books, without rules, to fish successfully, to the left or to the right, up or down stream, in the masterly manner that halts at no difficulty, then fish before, during and after a storm, when the clouds break and the sky is streaked with lightning, when the earth shakes with the grumbling thunder; it is then that, either through hunger or terror, all the fish forget their habits in a turbulent flight.

"In this confusion follow or neglect all favorable signs, and just go on fishing; you will march to victory!"

In order to catch fish of all sizes, he bought three well-perfected poles, made to be used as a cane in the city, which, on the river, could be transformed into a fishing rod by a simple jerk. He bought some number fifteen hooks for gudgeon, number twelve for bream, and with his number seven he expected to fill his basket with carp. He bought no earth worms because he was sure of finding them everywhere; but he laid in a provision of sand worms. He had a jar full of them, and in the evening he watched them with interest. The hideous creatures swarmed in their bath of bran as they do in putrid meat. Patissot wished to practice baiting his hook. He took up one with disgust, but he had hardly placed the curved steel point against it when it split open. Twenty times he repeated this without success, and he might have continued all night had he not feared to exhaust his supply of vermin.

He left by the first train. The station was full of people equipped with fishing lines. Some, like Patissot's, looked like simple bamboo canes; others, in one piece, pointed their slender ends to the skies. They looked like a forest of slender sticks, which mingled and clashed like swords or swayed like masts over an ocean of broad-brimmed straw hats.

When the train started fishing rods could be seen sticking out of all the windows and doors, giving to the train the appearance of a huge, bristly caterpillar winding through the fields.

Everybody got off at Courbevoie and rushed for the stage for Bezons. A crowd of fishermen crowded on top of the coach, holding their rods in their hands, giving the vehicle the appearance of a porcupine.

All along the road men were travelling in the same direction as though on a pilgrimage to an unknown Jerusalem. They were carrying those long, slender sticks resembling those carried by the faithful returning from Palestine. A tin box on a strap was fastened to their backs. They were in a hurry.

At Bezons the river appeared. People were lined along bath banks, men in frock coats, others in duck suits, others in blouses, women, children and even young girls of marriageable age; all were fishing.

Patissot started for the dam where his friend Boivin was waiting for him. The latter greeted him rather coolly. He had just made the acquaintance of a big, fat man of about fifty, who seemed very strong and whose skin was tanned. All three hired a big boat and lay off almost under the fall of the dam, where the fish are most plentiful.

Boivin was immediately ready. He baited his line and threw it out, and then sat motionless, watching the little float with extraordinary concentration. From time to time he would jerk his line out of the water and cast it farther out. The fat gentleman threw out his well-baited hooks, put his line down beside him, filled his pipe, lit it, crossed his arms, and, without another glance at the cork, he watched the water flow by. Patissot once more began trying to stick sand worms on his hooks. After about five minutes of this occupation he called to Boivin; "Monsieur Boivin, would you be so kind as to help me put these creatures on my hook? Try as I will, I can't seem to succeed." Boivin raised his head: "Please don't disturb me, Monsieur Patissot; we are not here for pleasure!" However, he baited the line, which Patissot then threw out, carefully imitating all the motions of his friend.

The boat was tossing wildly, shaken by the waves, and spun round like a top by the current, although anchored at both ends. Patissot, absorbed in the sport, felt a vague kind of uneasiness; he was uncomfortably heavy and somewhat dizzy.

They caught nothing. Little Boivin, very nervous, was gesticulating and shaking his head in despair. Patissot was as sad as though some disaster had overtaken him. The fat gentleman alone, still motionless, was quietly smoking without paying any attention to his line. At last Patissot, disgusted, turned toward him and said in a mournful voice:

"They are not biting, are they?"

He quietly replied:

"Of course not!"

Patissot surprised, looked at him.

"Do you ever catch many?"

"Never!"

"What! Never?"

The fat man, still smoking like a factory chimney, let out the following words, which completely upset his neighbor:

"It would bother me a lot if they did bite. I don't come here to fish; I come because I'm very comfortable here; I get shaken up as though I were at sea. If I take a line along, it's only to do as others do."

Monsieur Patissot, on the other hand, did not feel at all well. His discomfort, at first vague, kept increasing, and finally took on a definite form. He felt, indeed, as though he were being tossed by the sea, and he was suffering from seasickness. After the first attack had calmed down, he proposed leaving, but Boivin grew so furious that they almost came to blows. The fat man, moved by pity, rowed the boat back, and, as soon as Patissot had recovered from his seasickness, they bethought themselves of luncheon.

Two restaurants presented themselves. One of them, very small, looked like a beer garden, and was patronized by the poorer fishermen. The other one, which bore the imposing name of "Linden Cottage," looked like a middle-class residence and was frequented by the aristocracy of the rod. The two owners, born enemies, watched each other with hatred across a large field, which separated them, and where the white house of the dam keeper and of the inspector of the life-saving department stood out against the green grass. Moreover, these two officials disagreed, one of them upholding the beer garden and the other one defending the Elms, and the internal feuds which arose in these three houses reproduced the whole history of mankind.

Boivin, who knew the beer garden, wished to go there, exclaiming: "The food is very good, and it isn't expensive; you'll see. Anyhow, Monsieur Patissot, you needn't expect to get me tipsy the way you did last Sunday. My wife was furious, you know; and she has sworn never to forgive you!"

The fat gentleman declared that he would only eat at the Elms, because it was an excellent place and the cooking was as good as in the best restaurants in Paris.

"Do as you wish," declared Boivin; "I am going where I am accustomed to go." He left. Patissot, displeased at his friend's actions, followed the fat gentleman.

They ate together, exchanged ideas, discussed opinions and found that they were made for each other.

After the meal everyone started to fish again, but the two new friends left together. Following along the banks, they stopped near the railroad bridge and, still talking, they threw their lines in the water. The fish still refused to bite, but Patissot was now making the best of it.

A family was approaching. The father, whose whiskers stamped him as a judge, was holding an extraordinarily long rod; three boys of different sizes were carrying poles of different lengths, according to age; and the mother, who was very stout, gracefully manoeuvred a charming rod with a ribbon tied to the handle. The father bowed and asked:

"Is this spot good, gentlemen?" Patissot was going to speak, when his friend answered: "Fine!" The whole family smiled and settled down beside the fishermen. The Patissot was seized with a wild desire to catch a fish, just one, any kind, any size, in order to win the consideration of these people; so he began to handle his rod as he had seen Boivin do in the morning. He would let the cork follow the current to the end of the line, jerk the hooks out of the water, make them describe a large circle in the air and throw them out again a little higher up. He had even, as he thought, caught the knack of doing this movement gracefully. He had just jerked his line out rapidly when he felt it caught in something behind him. He tugged, and a scream burst from behind him. He perceived, caught on one of his hooks, and describing in the air a curve like a meteor, a magnificent hat which he placed right in the middle of the river.

He turned around, bewildered, dropping his pole, which followed the hat down the stream, while the fat gentleman, his new friend, lay on his back and roared with laughter. The lady, hatless and astounded, choked with anger; her husband was outraged and demanded the price of the hat, and Patissot paid about three times its value.

Then the family departed in a very dignified manner.

Patissot took another rod, and, until nightfall, he gave baths to sand worms. His neighbor was sleeping peacefully on the grass. Toward seven in the evening he awoke.

"Let's go away from here!" he said.

Then Patissot withdrew his line, gave a cry and sat down hard from astonishment. At the end of the string was a tiny little fish. When they looked at him more closely they found that he had been hooked through the stomach; the hook had caught him as it was being drawn out of the water.

Patissot was filled with a boundless, triumphant joy; he wished to have the fish fried for himself alone.

During the dinner the friends grew still more intimate. He learned that the fat gentleman lived at Argenteuil and had been sailing boats for thirty years without losing interest in the sport. He accepted to take luncheon with him the following Sunday and to take a sail in his friend's clipper, Plongeon. He became so interested in the conversation that he forgot all about his catch. He did not remember it until after the coffee, and he demanded that it be brought him. It was alone in the middle of a platter, and looked like a yellow, twisted match, But he ate it with pride and relish, and at night, on the omnibus, he told his neighbors that he had caught fourteen pounds of fish during the day.

TWO CELEBRITIES

Monsieur Patissot had promised his friend, the boating man, that he would spend the following Sunday with him. An unforeseen occurrence changed his plan. One evening, on the boulevard, he met one of his cousins whom he saw but very seldom. He was a pleasant journalist, well received in all classes of society, who offered to show Patissot many interesting things.

"What are you going to do next Sunday?"

"I'm going boating at Argenteuil."

"Come on! Boating is an awful bore; there is no variety to it. Listen —I'll take you along with me. I'll introduce you to two celebrities. We will visit the homes of two artists."

"But I have been ordered to go to the country!"

"That's just where we'll go. On the way we'll call on Meissonier, at his place in Poissy; then we'll walk over to Medan, where Zola lives. I have been commissioned to obtain his next novel for our newspaper."

Patissot, wild with joy, accepted the invitation. He even bought a new frock coat, as his own was too much worn to make a good appearance. He was terribly afraid of saying something foolish either to the artist or to the man of letters, as do people who speak of an art which they have never professed.

He mentioned his fears to his cousin, who laughed and answered: "Pshaw! Just pay them compliments, nothing but compliments, always compliments; in that way, if you say anything foolish it will be overlooked. Do you know Meissonier's paintings?"

"I should say I do."

"Have you read the Rougon-Macquart series?"

"From first to last."

"That's enough. Mention a painting from time to time, speak of a novel here and there and add:

"'Superb! Extraordinary! Delightful technique! Wonderfully powerful!' In that way you can always get along. I know that those two are very blasé about everything, but admiration always pleases an artist."

Sunday morning they left for Poissy.

Just a few steps from the station, at the end of the church square, they found Meissonier's property. After passing through a low door, painted red, which led into a beautiful alley of vines, the journalist stopped and, turning toward his companion, asked:

"What is your idea of Meissonier?"

Patissot hesitated. At last he decided: "A little man, well groomed, clean shaven, a soldierly appearance." The other smiled: "All right, come along." A quaint building in the form of a chalet appeared to the left; and to the right side, almost opposite, was the main house. It was a strange-looking building, where there was a mixture of everything, a mingling of Gothic fortress, manor, villa, hut, residence, cathedral, mosque, pyramid, a, weird combination of Eastern and Western architecture. The style was complicated enough to set a classical architect crazy, and yet there was something whimsical and pretty about it. It had been invented and built under the direction of the artist.

They went in; a collection of trunks encumbered a little parlor. A little man appeared, dressed in a jumper. The striking thing about him was his beard. He bowed to the journalist, and said: "My dear sir, I hope that you will excuse me; I only returned yesterday, and everything is all upset here. Please be seated." The other refused, excusing himself: "My dear master, I only dropped in to pay my respects while passing by." Patissot, very much embarrassed, was bowing at every word of his friend's, as though moving automatically, and he murmured, stammering: "What a su—su—superb property!" The artist, flattered, smiled, and suggested visiting it.

He led them first to a little pavilion of feudal aspect, where his former studio was. Then they crossed a parlor, a dining-room, a vestibule full of beautiful works of art, of beautiful Beauvais, Gobelin and Flanders tapestries. But the strange external luxury of ornamentation became, inside, a revel of immense stairways.

A magnificent grand stairway, a secret stairway in one tower, a servants' stairway in another, stairways everywhere! Patissot, by chance, opened a door and stepped back astonished. It was a veritable temple, this place of which respectable people only mention the name in English, an original and charming sanctuary in exquisite taste, fitted up like a pagoda, and the decoration of which must certainly have caused a great effort.

They next visited the park, which was complex, varied, with winding paths and full of old trees. But the journalist insisted on leaving; and, with many thanks, he took leave of the master: As they left they met a gardener; Patissot asked him: "Has Monsieur Meissonier owned this place for a long time?" The man answered: "Oh, monsieur! that needs explaining. I guess he bought the grounds in 1846. But, as for the house! he has already torn down and rebuilt that five or six times. It must have cost him at least two millions!" As Patissot left he was seized with an immense respect for this man, not on account of his success, glory or talent, but for putting so much money into a whim, because the bourgeois deprive themselves of all pleasure in order to hoard money.

After crossing Poissy, they struck out on foot along the road to Medan. The road first followed the Seine, which is dotted with charming islands at this place. Then they went up a hill and crossed the pretty village of Villaines, went down a little; and finally reached the neighborhood inhabited by the author of the Rougon-Macquart series.

A pretty old church with two towers appeared on the left. They walked along a short distance, and a passing farmer directed them to the writer's dwelling.

Before entering, they examined the house. A large building, square and new, very high, seemed, as in the fable of the mountain and the mouse, to have given birth to a tiny little white house, which nestled near it. This little house was the original dwelling, and had been built by the former owner. The tower had been erected by Zola.

They rang the bell. An enormous dog, a cross between a Saint Bernard and a Newfoundland, began to howl so terribly that Patissot felt a vague desire to retrace his steps. But a servant ran forward, calmed "Bertrand," opened the door, and took the journalist's card in order to carry it to his master.

"I hope that he will receive us!" murmured Patissot. "It would be too bad if we had come all this distance not to see him."

His companion smiled and answered: "Never fear, I have a plan for getting in."

But the servant, who had returned, simply asked them to follow him.

They entered the new building, and Patissot, who was quite enthusiastic, was panting as he climbed a stairway of ancient style which led to the second story.

At the same time he was trying to picture to himself this man whose glorious name echoes at present in all corners of the earth, amid the exasperated hatred of some, the real or feigned indignation of society, the envious scorn of several of his colleagues, the respect of a mass of readers, and the frenzied admiration of a great number. He expected to see a kind of bearded giant, of awe-inspiring aspect, with a thundering voice and an appearance little prepossessing at first.

The door opened on a room of uncommonly large dimensions, broad and high, lighted by an enormous window looking out over the valley. Old tapestries covered the walls; on the left, a monumental fireplace, flanked by two stone men, could have burned a century-old oak in one day. An immense table littered with books, papers and magazines stood in the middle of this apartment so vast and grand that it first engrossed the eye, and the attention was only afterward drawn to the man, stretched out when they entered on an Oriental divan where twenty persons could have slept. He took a few steps toward them, bowed, motioned to two seats, and turned back to his divan, where he sat with one leg drawn under him. A book lay open beside him, and in his right hand he held an ivory paper-cutter, the end of which he observed from time to time with one eye, closing the other with the persistency of a near-sighted person.

While the journalist explained the purpose of the visit, and the writer listened to him without yet answering, at times staring at him fixedly, Patissot, more and more embarrassed, was observing this celebrity.

Hardly forty, he was of medium height, fairly stout, and with a good-natured look. His head (very similar to those found in many Italian paintings of the sixteenth century), without being beautiful in the plastic sense of the word, gave an impression of great strength of character, power and intelligence. Short hair stood up straight on the high, well-developed forehead. A straight nose stopped short, as if cut off suddenly above the upper lip which was covered with a black mustache; over the whole chin was a closely-cropped beard. The dark, often ironical look was piercing, one felt that behind it there was a mind always actively at work observing people, interpreting words, analyzing gestures, uncovering the heart. This strong, round head was appropriate to his name, quick and short, with the bounding resonance of the two vowels.

When the journalist had fully explained his proposition, the writer answered him that he did not wish to make any definite arrangement, that he would, however, think the matter over, that his plans were not yet sufficiently defined. Then he stopped. It was a dismissal, and the two men, a little confused, arose. A desire seized Patissot; he wished this well-known person to say something to him, anything, some word which he could repeat to his colleagues; and, growing bold, he stammered: "Oh, monsieur! If you knew how I appreciate your works!" The other bowed, but answered nothing. Patissot became very bold and continued: "It is a great honor for me to speak to you to-day." The writer once more bowed, but with a stiff and impatient look. Patissot noticed it, and, completely losing his head, he added as he retreated: "What a su—su —superb property!"

Then, in the heart of the man of letters, the landowner awoke, and, smiling, he opened the window to show them the immense stretch of view. An endless horizon broadened out on all sides, giving a view of Triel, Pisse-Fontaine, Chanteloup, all the heights of Hautrie, and the Seine as far as the eye could see. The two visitors, delighted, congratulated him, and the house was opened to them. They saw everything, down to the dainty kitchen, whose walls and even ceilings were covered with porcelain tiles ornamented with blue designs, which excited the wonder of the farmers.

"How did you happen to buy this place?" asked the journalist.

The novelist explained that, while looking for a cottage to hire for the summer, he had found the little house, which was for sale for several thousand francs, a song, almost nothing. He immediately bought it.

"But everything that you have added must have cost you a good deal!"

The writer smiled, and answered: "Yes, quite a little."

The two men left. The journalist, taking Patissot by the arm, was philosophizing in a low voice:

"Every general has his Waterloo," he said; "every Balzac has his Jardies, and every artist living in the country feels like a landed proprietor."

They took the train at the station of Villaines, and, on the way home, Patissot loudly mentioned the names of the famous painter and of the great novelist as though they were his friends. He even allowed people to think that he had taken luncheon with one and dinner with the other.

BEFORE THE CELEBRATION

The celebration is approaching and preliminary quivers are already running through the streets, just as the ripples disturb the water preparatory to a storm. The shops, draped with flags, display a variety of gay-colored bunting materials, and the dry-goods people deceive one about the three colors as grocers do about the weight of candles. Little by little, hearts warm up to the matter; people speak about it in the street after dinner; ideas are exchanged:

"What a celebration it will be, my friend; what a celebration!"

"Have you heard the news? All the rulers are coming incognito, as bourgeois, in order to see it."

"I hear that the Emperor of Russia has arrived; he expects to go about everywhere with the Prince of Wales."

"It certainly will be a fine celebration!"

It is going to a celebration; what Monsieur Patissot, Parisian bourgeois, calls a celebration; one of these nameless tumults which, for fifteen hours, roll from one end of the city to the other, every ugly specimen togged out in its finest, a mob of perspiring bodies, where side by side are tossed about the stout gossip bedecked in red, white and blue ribbons, grown fat behind her counter and panting from lack of breath, the rickety clerk with his wife and brat in tow, the laborer carrying his youngster astride his neck, the bewildered provincial with his foolish, dazed expression, the groom, barely shaved and still spreading the perfume of the stable. And the foreigners dressed like monkeys, English women like giraffes, the water-carrier, cleaned up for the occasion, and the innumerable phalanx of little bourgeois, inoffensive little people, amused at everything. All this crowding and pressing, the sweat and dust, and the turmoil, all these eddies of human flesh, trampling of corns beneath the feet of your neighbors, this city all topsy-turvy, these vile odors, these frantic efforts toward nothing, the breath of millions of people, all redolent of garlic, give to Monsieur Patissot all the joy which it is possible for his heart to hold.

After reading the proclamation of the mayor on the walls of his district he had made his preparations.

This bit of prose said:

I wish to call your attention particularly to the part of

73

    individuals in this celebration. Decorate your homes, illuminate

    your windows. Get together, open up a subscription in order to give

    to your houses and to your street a more brilliant and more artistic

    appearance than the neighboring houses and streets.

Then Monsieur Patissot tried to imagine how he could give to his home an artistic appearance.

One serious obstacle stood in the way. His only window looked out on a courtyard, a narrow, dark shaft, where only the rats could have seen his three Japanese lanterns.

He needed a public opening. He found it. On the first floor of his house lived a rich man, a nobleman and a royalist, whose coachman, also a reactionary, occupied a garret-room on the sixth floor, facing the street. Monsieur Patissot supposed that by paying (every conscience can be bought) he could obtain the use of the room for the day. He proposed five francs to this citizen of the whip for the use of his room from noon till midnight. The offer was immediately accepted.

Then he began to busy himself with the decorations. Three flags, four lanterns, was that enough to give to this box an artistic appearance—to express all the noble feelings of his soul? No; assuredly not! But, notwithstanding diligent search and nightly meditation, Monsieur Patissot could think of nothing else. He consulted his neighbors, who were surprised at the question; he questioned his colleagues—every one had bought lanterns and flags, some adding, for the occasion, red, white and blue bunting.

Then he began to rack his brains for some original idea. He frequented the cafes, questioning the patrons; they lacked imagination. Then one morning he went out on top of an omnibus. A respectable-looking gentleman was smoking a cigar beside him, a little farther away a laborer was smoking his pipe upside down, near the driver two rough fellows were joking, and clerks of every description were going to business for three cents.

Before the stores stacks of flags were resplendent under the rising sun. Patissot turned to his neighbor.

"It is going to be a fine celebration," he said. The gentleman looked at him sideways and answered in a haughty manner:

"That makes no difference to me!"

"You are not going to take part in it?" asked the surprised clerk. The other shook his head disdainfully and declared:

"They make me tired with their celebrations! Whose celebration is it? The government's? I do not recognize this government, monsieur!"

But Patissot, as government employee, took on his superior manner, and answered in a stern voice:

"Monsieur, the Republic is the government."

His neighbor was not in the least disturbed, and, pushing his hands down in his pockets, he exclaimed:

"Well, and what then? It makes no difference to me. Whether it's for the Republic or something else, I don't care! What I want, monsieur, is to know my government. I saw Charles X. and adhered to him, monsieur; I saw Louis-Philippe and adhered to him, monsieur; I saw Napoleon and adhered to him; but I have never seen the Republic."

Patissot, still serious, answered:

"The Republic, monsieur, is represented by its president!"

The other grumbled:

"Well, them, show him to me!"

Patissot shrugged his shoulders.

"Every one can see him; he's not shut up in a closet!"

Suddenly the fat man grew angry.

"Excuse me, monsieur, he cannot be seen. I have personally tried more than a hundred times, monsieur. I have posted myself near the Elysee; he did not come out. A passer-by informed me that he was playing billiards in the cafe opposite; I went to the cafe opposite; he was not there. I had been promised that he would go to Melun for the convention; I went to Melun, I did not see him. At last I became weary. I did not even see Monsieur Gambetta, and I do not know a single deputy."

He was, growing excited:

"A government, monsieur, is made to be seen; that's what it's there for, and for nothing else. One must be able to know that on such and such a day at such an hour the government will pass through such and such a street. Then one goes there and is satisfied."

Patissot, now calm, was enjoying his arguments.

"It is true," he said, "that it is agreeable to know the people by whom one is governed."

The gentleman continued more gently:

"Do you know how I would manage the celebration? Well, monsieur, I would have a procession of gilded cars, like the chariots used at the crowning of kings; in them I would parade all the members of the government, from the president to the deputies, throughout Paris all day long. In that manner, at least, every one would know by sight the personnel of the state."

But one of the toughs near the coachman turned around, exclaiming:

"And the fatted ox, where would you put him?"

A laugh ran round the two benches. Patissot understood the objection, and murmured:

"It might not perhaps be very dignified."

The gentleman thought the matter over and admitted it.

"Then," he said, "I would place them in view some place, so that every one could see them without going out of his way; on the Triumphal Arch at the Place de l'Etoile, for instance; and I would have the whole population pass before them. That would be very imposing."

Once more the tough turned round and said:

"You'd have to take telescopes to see their faces."

The gentleman did not answer; he continued:

"It's just like the presentation of the flags! There ought to be some pretext, a mimic war ought to be organized, and the banners would be awarded to the troops as a reward. I had an idea about which I wrote to the minister; but he has not deigned to answer me. As the taking of the Bastille has been chosen for the date of the national celebration, a reproduction of this event might be made; there would be a pasteboard Bastille, fixed up by a scene-painter and concealing within its walls the whole Column of July. Then, monsieur, the troop would attack. That would be a magnificent spectacle as well as a lesson, to see the army itself overthrow the ramparts of tyranny. Then this Bastille would be set fire to and from the midst of the flames would appear the Column with the genius of Liberty, symbol of a new order and of the freedom of the people."

This time every one was listening to him and finding his idea excellent. An old gentleman exclaimed:

"That is a great idea, monsieur, which does you honor. It is to be regretted that the government did not adopt it."

A young man declared that actors ought to recite the "Iambes" of Barbier through the streets in order to teach the people art and liberty simultaneously.

These propositions excited general enthusiasm. Each one wished to have his word; all were wrought up. From a passing hand-organ a few strains of the Marseillaise were heard; the laborer started the song, and everybody joined in, roaring the chorus. The exalted nature of the song and its wild rhythm fired the driver, who lashed his horses to a gallop. Monsieur Patissot was bawling at the top of his lungs, and the passengers inside, frightened, were wondering what hurricane had struck them.

At last they stopped, and Monsieur Patissot, judging his neighbor to be a man of initiative, consulted him about the preparations which he expected to make:

"Lanterns and flags are all right,"' said Patissot; "but I prefer something better."

The other thought for a long time, but found nothing. Then, in despair, the clerk bought three flags and four lanterns.

AN EXPERIMENT IN LOVE

Many poets think that nature is incomplete without women, and hence, doubtless, come all the flowery comparisons which, in their songs, make our natural companion in turn a rose, a violet, a tulip, or something of that order. The need of tenderness which seizes us at dusk, when the evening mist begins to roll in from the hills, and when all the perfumes of the earth intoxicate us, is but imperfectly satisfied by lyric invocations. Monsieur Patissot, like all others, was seized with a wild desire for tenderness, for sweet kisses exchanged along a path where sunshine steals in at times, for the pressure of a pair of small hands, for a supple waist bending under his embrace.

He began to look at love as an unbounded pleasure, and, in his hours of reverie, he thanked the Great Unknown for having put so much charm into the caresses of human beings. But he needed a companion, and he did not know where to find one. On the advice of a friend, he went to the Folies-Bergere. There he saw a complete assortment. He was greatly perplexed to choose between them, for the desires of his heart were chiefly composed of poetic impulses, and poetry did not seem to be the strong point of these young ladies with penciled eyebrows who smiled at him in such a disturbing manner, showing the enamel of their false teeth. At last his choice fell on a young beginner who seemed poor and timid and whose sad look seemed to announce a nature easily influenced by poetry.

He made an appointment with her for the following day at nine o'clock at the Saint-Lazare station. She did not come, but she was kind enough to send a friend in her stead.

She was a tall, red-haired girl, patriotically dressed in three colors, and covered by an immense tunnel hat, of which her head occupied the centre. Monsieur Patissot, a little disappointed, nevertheless accepted this substitute. They left for Maisons-Laffite, where regattas and a grand Venetian festival had been announced.

As soon as they were in the car, which was already occupied by two gentlemen who wore the red ribbon and three ladies who must at least have been duchesses, they were so dignified, the big red-haired girl, who answered the name of Octavie, announced to Patissot, in a screeching voice, that she was a fine girl fond of a good time and loving the country because there she could pick flowers and eat fried fish. She laughed with a shrillness which almost shattered the windows, familiarly calling her companion "My big darling."

Shame overwhelmed Patissot, who as a government employee, had to observe a certain amount of decorum. But Octavie stopped talking, glancing at her neighbors, seized with the overpowering desire which haunts all women of a certain class to make the acquaintance of respectable women. After about five minutes she thought she had found an opening, and, drawing from her pocket a Gil-Blas, she politely offered it to one of the amazed ladies, who declined, shaking her head. Then the big, red-haired girl began saying things with a double meaning, speaking of women who are stuck up without being any better than the others; sometimes she would let out a vulgar word which acted like a bomb exploding amid the icy dignity of the passengers.

At last they arrived. Patissot immediately wished to gain the shady nooks of the park, hoping that the melancholy of the forest would quiet the ruffled temper of his companion. But an entirely different effect resulted. As soon as she was amid the leaves and grass she began to sing at the top of her lungs snatches from operas which had stuck in her frivolous mind, warbling and trilling, passing from "Robert le Diable" to the "Muette," lingering especially on a sentimental love-song, whose last verses she sang in a voice as piercing as a gimlet.

Then suddenly she grew hungry. Patissot, who was still awaiting the hoped-for tenderness, tried in vain to retain her. Then she grew angry, exclaiming:

"I am not here for a dull time, am I?"

He had to take her to the Petit-Havre restaurant, which was near the place where the regatta was to be held.

She ordered an endless luncheon, a succession of dishes substantial enough to feed a regiment. Then, unable to wait, she called for relishes. A box of sardines was brought; she started in on it as though she intended to swallow the box itself. But when she had eaten two or three of the little oily fish she declared that she was no longer hungry and that she wished to see the preparations for the race.

Patissot, in despair and in his turn seized with hunger, absolutely refused to move. She started off alone, promising to return in time for the dessert. He began to eat in lonely silence, not knowing how to lead this rebellious nature to the realization of his dreams.

As she did not return he set out in search of her. She had found some friends, a troop of boatmen, in scanty garb, sunburned to the tips of their ears, and gesticulating, who were loudly arranging the details of the race in front of the house of Fourmaise, the builder.

Two respectable-looking gentlemen, probably the judges, were listening attentively. As soon as she saw Patissot, Octavie, who was leaning on the tanned arm of a strapping fellow who probably had more muscle than brains, whispered a few words in his ears. He answered:

"That's an agreement."

She returned to the clerk full of joy, her eyes sparkling, almost caressing.

"Let's go for a row," said she.

Pleased to see her so charming, he gave in to this new whim and procured a boat. But she obstinately refused to go to the races, notwithstanding Patissot's wishes.

"I had rather be alone with you, darling."

His heart thrilled. At last!

He took off his coat and began to row madly.

An old dilapidated mill, whose worm-eaten wheels hung over the water, stood with its two arches across a little arm of the river. Slowly they passed beneath it, and, when they were on the other side, they noticed before them a delightful little stretch of river, shaded by great trees which formed an arch over their heads. The little stream flowed along, winding first to the right and then to the left, continually revealing new scenes, broad fields on one side and on the other side a hill covered with cottages. They passed before a bathing establishment almost entirely hidden by the foliage, a charming country spot where gentlemen in clean gloves and beribboned ladies displayed all the ridiculous awkwardness of elegant people in the country. She cried joyously:

"Later on we will take a dip there."

Farther on, in a kind of bay, she wished to stop, coaxing:

"Come here, honey, right close to me."

She put her arm around his neck and, leaning her head on his shoulder, she murmured:

"How nice it is! How delightful it is on the water!"

Patissot was reveling in happiness. He was thinking of those foolish boatmen who, without ever feeling the penetrating charm of the river banks and the delicate grace of the reeds, row along out of breath, perspiring and tired out, from the tavern where they take luncheon to the tavern where they take dinner.

He was so comfortable that he fell asleep. When he awoke, he was alone. He called, but no one answered. Anxious, he climbed up on the side of the river, fearing that some accident might have happened.

Then, in the distance, coming in his direction, he saw a long, slender gig which four oarsmen as black as negroes were driving through the water like an arrow. It came nearer, skimming over the water; a woman was holding the tiller. Heavens! It looked—it was she! In order to regulate the rhythm of the stroke, she was singing in her shrill voice a boating song, which she interrupted for a minute as she got in front of Patissot. Then, throwing him a kiss, she cried:

"You big goose!"

A DINNER AND SOME OPINIONS

On the occasion of the national celebration Monsieur Antoine Perdrix, chief of Monsieur Patissot's department, was made a knight of the Legion of Honor. He had been in service for thirty years under preceding governments, and for ten years under the present one. His employees, although grumbling a little at being thus rewarded in the person of their chief, thought it wise, nevertheless, to offer him a cross studded with paste diamonds. The new knight, in turn, not wishing to be outdone, invited them all to dinner for the following Sunday, at his place at Asnieres.

The house, decorated with Moorish ornaments, looked like a cafe concert, but its location gave it value, as the railroad cut through the whole garden, passing within a hundred and fifty feet of the porch. On the regulation plot of grass stood a basin of Roman cement, containing goldfish and a stream of water the size of that which comes from a syringe, which occasionally made microscopic rainbows at which the guests marvelled.

The feeding of this irrigator was the constant preoccupation of Monsieur Perdrix, who would sometimes get up at five o'clock in the morning in order to fill the tank. Then, in his shirt sleeves, his big stomach almost bursting from his trousers, he would pump wildly, so that on returning from the office he could have the satisfaction of letting the fountain play and of imagining that it was cooling off the garden.

On the night of the official dinner all the guests, one after the other, went into ecstasies over the surroundings, and each time they heard a train in the distance, Monsieur Perdrix would announce to them its destination: Saint-Germain, Le Havre, Cherbourg, or Dieppe, and they would playfully wave to the passengers leaning from the windows.

The whole office force was there. First came Monsieur Capitaine, the assistant chief; Monsieur Patissot, chief clerk; then Messieurs de Sombreterre and Vallin, elegant young employees who only came to the office when they had to; lastly Monsieur Rade, known throughout the ministry for the absurd doctrines which he upheld, and the copying clerk, Monsieur Boivin.

Monsieur Rade passed for a character. Some called him a dreamer or an idealist, others a revolutionary; every one agreed that he was very clumsy. Old, thin and small, with bright eyes and long, white hair, he had all his life professed a profound contempt for administrative work. A book rummager and a great reader, with a nature continually in revolt against everything, a seeker of truth and a despiser of popular prejudices, he had a clear and paradoxical manner of expressing his opinions which closed the mouths of self-satisfied fools and of those that were discontented without knowing why. People said: "That old fool of a Rade," or else: "That harebrained Rade"; and the slowness, of his promotion seemed to indicate the reason, according to commonplace minds. His freedom of speech often made—his colleagues tremble; they asked themselves with terror how he had been able to keep his place as long as he had. As soon as they had seated themselves, Monsieur Perdrix thanked his "collaborators" in a neat little speech, promising them his protection, the more valuable as his power grew, and he ended with a stirring peroration in which he thanked and glorified a government so liberal and just that it knows how to seek out the worthy from among the humble.

Monsieur Capitaine, the assistant chief, answered in the name of the office, congratulated, greeted, exalted, sang the praises of all; frantic applause greeted these two bits of eloquence. After that they settled down seriously to the business of eating.

Everything went well up to the dessert; lack of conversation went unnoticed. But after the coffee a discussion arose, and Monsieur Rade let himself loose and soon began to overstep the bounds of discretion.

They naturally discussed love, and a breath of chivalry intoxicated this room full of bureaucrats; they praised and exalted the superior beauty of woman, the delicacy of her soul, her aptitude for exquisite things, the correctness of her judgment, and the refinement of her sentiments. Monsieur Rade began to protest, energetically refusing to credit the so-called "fair" sex with all the qualities they ascribed to it; then, amidst the general indignation, he quoted some authors:

"Schopenhauer, gentlemen, Schopenhauer, the great philosopher, revered by all Germany, says: 'Man's intelligence must have been terribly deadened by love in order to call this sex with the small waist, narrow shoulders, large hips and crooked legs, the fair sex. All its beauty lies in the instinct of love. Instead of calling it the fair, it would have been better to call it the unaesthetic sex. Women have neither the appreciation nor the knowledge of music, any more than they have of poetry or of the plastic arts; with them it is merely an apelike imitation, pure pretence, affectation cultivated from their desire to please.'"

"The man who said that is an idiot," exclaimed Monsieur de Sombreterre.

Monsieur Rade smilingly continued:

"And how about Rousseau, gentlemen? Here is his opinion: 'Women, as a rule, love no art, are skilled in none, and have no talent.'"

Monsieur de Sombreterre disdainfully shrugged his shoulders:

"Then Rousseau is as much of a fool as the other, that's all."

Monsieur Rade, still smiling, went on:

"And this is what Lord Byron said, who, nevertheless, loved women: 'They should be well fed and well dressed, but not allowed to mingle with society. They should also be taught religion, but they should ignore poetry and politics, only being allowed to read religious works or cook-books.'"

Monsieur Rade continued:

"You see, gentlemen, all of them study painting and music. But not a single one of them has ever painted a remarkable picture or composed a great opera! Why, gentlemen? Because they are the 'sexes sequior', the secondary sex in every sense of the word, made to be kept apart, in the background."

Monsieur Patissot was growing angry, and exclaimed:

"And how about Madame Sand, monsieur?"

"She is the one exception, monsieur, the one exception. I will quote to you another passage from another great philosopher, this one an Englishman, Herbert Spencer. Here is what he says: 'Each sex is capable, under the influence of abnormal stimulation, of manifesting faculties ordinarily reserved for the other one. Thus, for instance, in extreme cases a special excitement may cause the breasts of men to give milk; children deprived of their mothers have often thus been saved in time of famine. Nevertheless, we do not place this faculty of giving milk among the male attributes. It is the same with female intelligence, which, in certain cases, will give superior products, but which is not to be considered in an estimate of the feminine nature as a social factor.'"

All Monsieur Patissot's chivalric instincts were wounded and he declared:

"You are not a Frenchman, monsieur. French gallantry is a form of patriotism."

Monsieur Rade retorted:

"I have very little patriotism, monsieur, as little as I can get along with."

A coolness settled over the company, but he continued quietly:

"Do you admit with me that war is a barbarous thing; that this custom of killing off people constitutes a condition of savagery; that it is odious, when life is the only real good, to see governments, whose duty is to protect the lives of their subjects, persistently looking for means of destruction? Am I not right? Well, if war is a terrible thing, what about patriotism, which is the idea at the base of it? When a murderer kills he has a fixed idea; it is to steal. When a good man sticks his bayonet through another good man, father of a family, or, perhaps, a great artist, what idea is he following out?"

Everybody was shocked.

"When one has such thoughts, one should not express them in public."

M. Patissot continued:

"There are, however, monsieur, principles which all good people recognize."

M. Rade asked: "Which ones?"

Then very solemnly, M. Patissot pronounced: "Morality, monsieur."

M. Rade was beaming; he exclaimed:

"Just let me give you one example, gentlemen, one little example. What is your opinion of the gentlemen with the silk caps who thrive along the boulevard's on the delightful traffic which you know, and who make a living out of it?"

A look of disgust ran round the table:

"Well, gentlemen! only a century ago, when an elegant gentleman, very ticklish about his honor, had for—friend—a beautiful and rich lady, it was considered perfectly proper to live at her expense and even to squander her whole fortune. This game was considered delightful. This only goes to show that the principles of morality are by no means settled—and that—"

M. Perdrix, visibly embarrassed, stopped him:

"M. Rade, you are sapping the very foundations of society. One must always have principles. Thus, in politics, here is M. de Sombreterre, who is a Legitimist; M. Vallin, an Orleanist; M. Patissot and myself, Republicans; we all have very different principles, and yet we agree very well because we have them."

But M. Rade exclaimed:

"I also have principles, gentlemen, very distinct ones."

M. Patissot raised his head and coldly asked:

"It would please me greatly to know them, monsieur."

M. Rade did not need to be coaxed.

"Here they are, monsieur:

"First principle—Government by one person is a monstrosity.

"Second principle—Restricted suffrage is an injustice.

"Third principle—Universal suffrage is idiotic.

"To deliver up millions of men, superior minds, scientists, even geniuses, to the caprice and will of a being who, in an instant of gaiety, madness, intoxication or love, would not hesitate to sacrifice everything for his exalted fancy, would spend the wealth of the country amassed by others with difficulty, would have thousands of men slaughtered on the battle-fields, all this appears to me—a simple logician—a monstrous aberration.

"But, admitting that a country must govern itself, to exclude, on some always debatable pretext, a part of the citizens from the administration of affairs is such an injustice that it seems to me unworthy of a further discussion.

"There remains universal suffrage. I suppose that you will agree with me that geniuses are a rarity. Let us be liberal and say that there are at present five in France. Now, let us add, perhaps, two hundred men with a decided talent, one thousand others possessing various talents, and ten thousand superior intellects. This is a staff of eleven thousand two hundred and five minds. After that you have the army of mediocrities followed by the multitude of fools. As the mediocrities and the fools always form the immense majority, it is impossible for them to elect an intelligent government.

"In order to be fair I admit that logically universal suffrage seems to me the only admissible principle, but it is impracticable. Here are the reasons why:

"To make all the living forces of the country cooperate in the government, to represent all the interests, to take into account all the rights, is an ideal dream, but hardly practicable, because the only force which can be measured is that very one which should be neglected, the stupid strength of numbers, According to your method, unintelligent numbers equal genius, knowledge, learning, wealth and industry. When you are able to give to a member of the Institute ten thousand votes to a ragman's one, one hundred votes for a great land-owner as against his farmer's ten, then you will have approached an equilibrium of forces and obtained a national representation which will really represent the strength of the nation. But I challenge you to do it.

"Here are my conclusions:

"Formerly, when a man was a failure at every other profession he turned photographer; now he has himself elected a deputy. A government thus composed will always be sadly lacking, incapable of evil as well as of good. On the other hand, a despot, if he be stupid, can do a lot of harm, and, if he be intelligent (a thing which is very scarce), he may do good.

"I cannot decide between these two forms of government; I declare myself to be an anarchist, that is to say, a partisan of that power which is the most unassuming, the least felt, the most liberal, in the broadest sense of the word, and revolutionary at the same time; by that I mean the everlasting enemy of this same power, which can in no way be anything but defective. That's all!"

Cries of indignation rose about the table, and all, whether Legitimist, Orleanist or Republican through force of circumstances, grew red with anger. M. Patissot especially was choking with rage, and, turning toward M. Rade, he cried:

"Then, monsieur, you believe in nothing?"

The other answered quietly:

"You're absolutely correct, monsieur."

The anger felt by all the guests prevented M. Rade from continuing, and M. Perdrix, as chief, closed the discussion.

"Enough, gentlemen! We each have our opinion, and we have no intention of changing it."

All agreed with the wise words. But M. Rade, never satisfied, wished to have the last word.

"I have, however, one moral," said he. "It is simple and always applicable. One sentence embraces the whole thought; here it is: 'Never do unto another that which you would not have him do unto you.' I defy you to pick any flaw in it, while I will undertake to demolish your most sacred principles with three arguments."

This time there was no answer. But as they were going home at night, by couples, each one was saying to his companion: "Really,

M. Rade goes much too far. His mind must surely be unbalanced. He ought to be appointed assistant chief at the Charenton Asylum."

A RECOLLECTION

How many recollections of youth come to me in the soft sunlight of early spring! It was an age when all was pleasant, cheerful, charming, intoxicating. How exquisite are the remembrances of those old springtimes!

Do you recall, old friends and brothers, those happy years when life was nothing but a triumph and an occasion for mirth? Do you recall the days of wanderings around Paris, our jolly poverty, our walks in the fresh, green woods, our drinks in the wine-shops on the banks of the Seine and our commonplace and delightful little flirtations?

I will tell you about one of these. It was twelve years ago and already appears to me so old, so old that it seems now as if it belonged to the other end of life, before middle age, this dreadful middle age from which I suddenly perceived the end of the journey.

I was then twenty-five. I had just come to Paris. I was in a government office, and Sundays were to me like unusual festivals, full of exuberant happiness, although nothing remarkable occurred.

Now it is Sunday every day, but I regret the time when I had only one Sunday in the week. How enjoyable it was! I had six francs to spend!

On this particular morning I awoke with that sense of freedom that all clerks know so well—the sense of emancipation, of rest, of quiet and of independence.

I opened my window. The weather was charming. A blue sky full of sunlight and swallows spread above the town.

I dressed quickly and set out, intending to spend the day in the woods breathing the air of the green trees, for I am originally a rustic, having been brought up amid the grass and the trees.

Paris was astir and happy in the warmth and the light. The front of the houses was bathed in sunlight, the janitress' canaries were singing in their cages and there was an air of gaiety in the streets, in the faces of the inhabitants, lighting them up with a smile as if all beings and all things experienced a secret satisfaction at the rising of the brilliant sun.

I walked towards the Seine to take the Swallow, which would land me at Saint-Cloud.

How I loved waiting for the boat on the wharf:

It seemed to me that I was about to set out for the ends of the world, for new and wonderful lands. I saw the boat approaching yonder, yonder under the second bridge, looking quite small with its plume of smoke, then growing larger and ever larger, as it drew near, until it looked to me like a mail steamer.

It came up to the wharf and I went on board. People were there already in their Sunday clothes, startling toilettes, gaudy ribbons and bright scarlet designs. I took up a position in the bows, standing up and looking at the quays, the trees, the houses and the bridges disappearing behind us. And suddenly I perceived the great viaduct of Point du Jour which blocked the river. It was the end of Paris, the beginning of the country, and behind the double row of arches the Seine, suddenly spreading out as though it had regained space and liberty, became all at once the peaceful river which flows through the plains, alongside the wooded hills, amid the meadows, along the edge of the forests.

After passing between two islands the Swallow went round a curved verdant slope dotted with white houses. A voice called out: "Bas Meudon" and a little further on, "Sevres," and still further, "Saint-Cloud."

I went on shore and walked hurriedly through the little town to the road leading to the wood.

I had brought with me a map of the environs of Paris, so that I might not lose my way amid the paths which cross in every direction these little forests where Parisians take their outings.

As soon as I was unperceived I began to study my guide, which seemed to be perfectly clear. I was to turn to the right, then to the left, then again to the left and I should reach Versailles by evening in time for dinner.

I walked slowly beneath the young leaves, drinking in the air, fragrant with the odor of young buds and sap. I sauntered along, forgetful of musty papers, of the offices, of my chief, my colleagues, my documents, and thinking of the good things that were sure to come to me, of all the veiled unknown contained in the future. A thousand recollections of childhood came over me, awakened by these country odors, and I walked along, permeated with the fragrant, living enchantment, the emotional enchantment of the woods warmed by the sun of June.

At times I sat down to look at all sorts of little flowers growing on a bank, with the names of which I was familiar. I recognized them all just as if they were the ones I had seen long ago in the country. They were yellow, red, violet, delicate, dainty, perched on long stems or close to the ground. Insects of all colors and shapes, short, long, of peculiar form, frightful, and microscopic monsters, climbed quietly up the stalks of grass which bent beneath their weight.

Then I went to sleep for some hours in a hollow and started off again, refreshed by my doze.

In front of me lay an enchanting pathway and through its somewhat scanty foliage the sun poured down drops of light on the marguerites which grew there. It stretched out interminably, quiet and deserted, save for an occasional big wasp, who would stop buzzing now and then to sip from a flower, and then continue his way.

All at once I perceived at the end of the path two persons, a man and a woman, coming towards me. Annoyed at being disturbed in my quiet walk, I was about to dive into the thicket, when I thought I heard someone calling me. The woman was, in fact, shaking her parasol, and the man, in his shirt sleeves, his coat over one arm, was waving the other as a signal of distress.

I went towards them. They were walking hurriedly, their faces very red, she with short, quick steps and he with long strides. They both looked annoyed and fatigued.

The woman asked:

"Can you tell me, monsieur, where we are? My fool of a husband made us lose our way, although he pretended he knew the country perfectly."

I replied confidently:

"Madame, you are going towards Saint-Cloud and turning your back on Versailles."

With a look of annoyed pity for her husband, she exclaimed:

"What, we are turning our back on Versailles? Why, that is just where we want to dine!"

"I am going there also, madame."

"Mon Dieu, mon Dieu, mon Dieu!" she repeated, shrugging her shoulders, and in that tone of sovereign contempt assumed by women to express their exasperation.

She was quite young, pretty, a brunette with a slight shadow on her upper lip.

As for him, he was perspiring and wiping his forehead. It was assuredly a little Parisian bourgeois couple. The man seemed cast down, exhausted and distressed.

"But, my dear friend, it was you—" he murmured.

She did not allow him to finish his sentence.

"It was I! Ah, it is my fault now! Was it I who wanted to go out without getting any information, pretending that I knew how to find my way? Was it I who wanted to take the road to the right on top of the hill, insisting that I recognized the road? Was it I who undertook to take charge of Cachou—"

She had not finished speaking when her husband, as if he had suddenly gone crazy, gave a piercing scream, a long, wild cry that could not be described in any language, but which sounded like 'tuituit'.

The young woman did not appear to be surprised or moved and resumed:

"No, really, some people are so stupid and they pretend they know everything. Was it I who took the train to Dieppe last year instead of the train to Havre—tell me, was it I? Was it I who bet that M. Letourneur lived in Rue des Martyres? Was it I who would not believe that Celeste was a thief?"

She went on, furious, with a surprising flow of language, accumulating the most varied, the most unexpected and the most overwhelming accusations drawn from the intimate relations of their daily life, reproaching her husband for all his actions, all his ideas, all his habits, all his enterprises, all his efforts, for his life from the time of their marriage up to the present time.

He strove to check her, to calm her and stammered:

"But, my dear, it is useless—before monsieur. We are making ourselves ridiculous. This does not interest monsieur."

And he cast mournful glances into the thicket as though he sought to sound its peaceful and mysterious depths, in order to flee thither, to escape and hide from all eyes, and from time to time he uttered a fresh scream, a prolonged and shrill "tuituit." I took this to be a nervous affection.

The young woman, suddenly turning towards me: and changing her tone with singular rapidity, said:

"If monsieur will kindly allow us, we will accompany him on the road, so as not to lose our way again, and be obliged, possibly, to sleep in the wood."

I bowed. She took my arm and began to talk about a thousand things —about herself, her life, her family, her business. They were glovers in the Rue Saint-Lazare.

Her husband walked beside her, casting wild glances into the thick wood and screaming "tuituit" every few moments.

At last I inquired:

"Why do you scream like that?"

"I have lost my poor dog," he replied in a tone of discouragement and despair.

"How is that—you have lost your dog?"

"Yes. He was just a year old. He had never been outside the shop. I wanted to take him to have a run in the woods. He had never seen the grass nor the leaves and he was almost wild. He began to run about and bark and he disappeared in the wood. I must also add that he was greatly afraid of the train. That may have driven him mad. I kept on calling him, but he has not come back. He will die of hunger in there."

Without turning towards her husband, the young woman said:

"If you had left his chain on, it would not have happened. When people are as stupid as you are they do not keep a dog."

"But, my dear, it was you—" he murmured timidly.

She stopped short, and looking into his eyes as if she were going to tear them out, she began again to cast in his face innumerable reproaches.

It was growing dark. The cloud of vapor that covers the country at dusk was slowly rising and there was a poetry in the air, induced by the peculiar and enchanting freshness of the atmosphere that one feels in the woods at nightfall.

Suddenly the young man stopped, and feeling his body feverishly, exclaimed:

"Oh, I think that I—"

She looked at him.

"Well, what?"

"I did not notice that I had my coat on my arm."

"Well—?"

"I have lost my pocketbook—my money was in it."

She shook with anger and choked with indignation.

"That was all that was lacking. How stupid you are! how stupid you are! Is it possible that I could have married such an idiot! Well, go and look for it, and see that you find it. I am going on to Versailles with monsieur. I do not want to sleep in the wood."

"Yes, my dear," he replied gently. "Where shall I find you?"

A restaurant had been recommended to me. I gave him the address.

He turned back and, stooping down as he searched the ground with anxious eyes, he moved away, screaming "tuituit" every few moments.

We could see him for some time until the growing darkness concealed all but his outline, but we heard his mournful "tuituit," shriller and shriller as the night grew darker.

As for me, I stepped along quickly and happily in the soft twilight, with this little unknown woman leaning on my arm. I tried to say pretty things to her, but could think of nothing. I remained silent, disturbed, enchanted.

Our path was suddenly crossed by a high road. To the right I perceived a town lying in a valley.

What was this place? A man was passing. I asked him. He replied:

"Bougival."

I was dumfounded.

"What, Bougival? Are you sure?"

"Parbleu, I belong there!"

The little woman burst into an idiotic laugh.

I proposed that we should take a carriage and drive to Versailles. She replied:

"No, indeed. This is very funny and I am very hungry. I am really quite calm. My husband will find his way all right. It is a treat to me to be rid of him for a few hours."

We went into a restaurant beside the water and I ventured to ask for a private compartment. We had some supper. She sang, drank champagne, committed all sorts of follies.

That was my first serious flirtation.

OUR LETTERS

ight hours of railway travel induce sleep for some persons and insomnia for others; with me, any journey prevents my sleeping on the following night.

At about five o'clock I arrived at the estate of Abelle, which belongs to my friends, the Murets d'Artus, to spend three weeks there. It is a pretty house, built by one of their grandfathers in the style of the latter half of the last century. Therefore it has that intimate character of dwellings that have always been inhabited, furnished and enlivened by the same people. Nothing changes; nothing alters the soul of the dwelling, from which the furniture has never been taken out, the tapestries never unnailed, thus becoming worn out, faded, discolored, on the same walls. None of the old furniture leaves the place; only from time to time it is moved a little to make room for a new piece, which enters there like a new-born infant in the midst of brothers and sisters.

The house is on a hill in the center of a park which slopes down to the river, where there is a little stone bridge. Beyond the water the fields stretch out in the distance, and here one can see the cows wandering around, pasturing on the moist grass; their eyes seem full of the dew, mist and freshness of the pasture. I love this dwelling, just as one loves a thing which one ardently desires to possess. I return here every autumn with infinite delight; I leave with regret.

After I had dined with this friendly family, by whom I was received like a relative, I asked my friend, Paul Muret: "Which room did you give me this year?"

"Aunt Rose's room."

An hour later, followed by her three children, two little girls and a boy, Madame Muret d'Artus installed me in Aunt Rose's room, where I had not yet slept.

When I was alone I examined the walls, the furniture, the general aspect of the room, in order to attune my mind to it. I knew it but little, as I had entered it only once or twice, and I looked indifferently at a pastel portrait of Aunt Rose, who gave her name to the room.

This old Aunt Rose, with her curls, looking at me from behind the glass, made very little impression on my mind. She looked to me like a woman of former days, with principles and precepts as strong on the maxims of morality as on cooking recipes, one of these old aunts who are the bugbear of gaiety and the stern and wrinkled angel of provincial families.

I never had heard her spoken of; I knew nothing of her life or of her death. Did she belong to this century or to the preceding one? Had she left this earth after a calm or a stormy existence? Had she given up to heaven the pure soul of an old maid, the calm soul of a spouse, the tender one of a mother, or one moved by love? What difference did it make? The name alone, "Aunt Rose," seemed ridiculous, common, ugly.

I picked up a candle and looked at her severe face, hanging far up in an old gilt frame. Then, as I found it insignificant, disagreeable, even unsympathetic, I began to examine the furniture. It dated from the period of Louis XVI, the Revolution and the Directorate. Not a chair, not a curtain had entered this room since then, and it gave out the subtle odor of memories, which is the combined odor of wood, cloth, chairs, hangings, peculiar to places wherein have lived hearts that have loved and suffered.

I retired but did not sleep. After I had tossed about for an hour or two, I decided to get up and write some letters.

I opened a little mahogany desk with brass trimmings, which was placed between the two windows, in hope of finding some ink and paper; but all I found was a quill-pen, very much worn, and chewed at the end. I was about to close this piece of furniture, when a shining spot attracted my attention it looked like the yellow head of a nail. I scratched it with my finger, and it seemed to move. I seized it between two finger-nails, and pulled as hard as I could. It came toward me gently. It was a long gold pin which had been slipped into a hole in the wood and remained hidden there.

Why? I immediately thought that it must have served to work some spring which hid a secret, and I looked. It took a long time. After about two hours of investigation, I discovered another hole opposite the first one, but at the bottom of a groove. Into this I stuck my pin: a little shelf sprang toward my face, and I saw two packages of yellow letters, tied with a blue ribbon.

I read them. Here are two of them:

So you wish me to return to you your letters, my dearest friend.

Here they are, but it pains me to obey. Of what are you afraid?

That I might lose them? But they are under lock and key. Do you fear that they might be stolen? I guard against that, for they are my dearest treasure.

Yes, it pains me deeply. I wondered whether, perhaps you might not be feeling some regret! Not regret at having loved me, for I know that you still do, but the regret of having expressed on white paper this living love in hours when your heart did not confide in me, but in the pen that you held in your hand. When we love, we have need of confession, need of talking or writing, and we either talk or write. Words fly away, those sweet words made of music, air and tenderness, warm and light, which escape as soon as they are uttered, which remain in the memory alone, but which one can neither
see, touch nor kiss, as one can with the words written by your hand.

Your letters? Yes, I am returning them to you! But with what sorrow!

Undoubtedly, you must have had an after thought of delicate shame at
expressions that are ineffaceable. In your sensitive and timid soul you must have regretted having written to a man that you loved him.
You remembered sentences that called up recollections, and you said to yourself: "I will make ashes of those words."

Be satisfied, be calm. Here are your letters. I love you.
MY FRIEND:

No, you have not understood me, you have not guessed. I do not regret, and I never shall, that I told you of my affection.

I will always write to you, but you must return my letters to me as soon as you have read them.

I shall shock you, my friend, when I tell you the reason for this demand. It is not poetic, as you imagined, but practical. I am afraid, not of you, but of some mischance. I am guilty. I do not wish my fault to affect others than myself.

Understand me well. You and I may both die. You might fall off your horse, since you ride every day; you might die from a sudden attack, from a duel, from heart disease, from a carriage accident, in a thousand ways. For, if there is only one death, there are more ways of its reaching us than there are days or us to live.

Then your sisters, your brother, or your sister-in-law might find my letters! Do you think that they love me? I doubt it. And then, even if they adored me, is it possible for two women and one man to know a secret—such a secret!—and not to tell of it?

I seem to be saying very disagreeable things, speaking first of your death, and then suspecting the discreetness of your relatives.

But don't all of us die sooner or later? And it is almost certain that one of us will precede the other under the ground. We must therefore foresee all dangers, even that one.

As for me, I will keep your letters beside mine, in the secret of my little desk. I will show them to you there, sleeping side by side in their silken hiding place, full of our love, like lovers in a tomb.

You will say to me: "But if you should die first, my dear, your husband will find these letters."

Oh! I fear nothing. First of all, he does not know the secret of my desk, and then he will not look for it. And even if he finds it after my death, I fear nothing.

Did you ever stop to think of all the love letters that have been found after death? I have been thinking of this for a long time, and that is the reason I decided to ask you for my letters.

Think that never, do you understand, never, does a woman burn, tear or destroy the letters in which it is told her that she is loved. That is our whole life, our whole hope, expectation and dream. These little papers which bear our name in caressing terms are relics which we adore; they are chapels in which we are the saints. Our love letters are our titles to beauty, grace, seduction, the intimate vanity of our womanhood; they are the treasures of our heart. No, a woman does not destroy these secret and delicious archives of her life.

But, like everybody else, we die, and then—then these letters are found! Who finds them? The husband. Then what does he do? Nothing. He burns them.

Oh, I have thought a great deal about that! Just think that every day women are dying who have been loved; every day the traces and proofs of their fault fall into the hands of their husbands, and that there is never a scandal, never a duel.

Think, my dear, of what a man's heart is. He avenges himself on a living woman; he fights with the man who has dishonored her, kills him while she lives, because, well, why? I do not know exactly why. But, if, after her death, he finds similar proofs, he burns them and no one is the wiser, and he continues to shake hands with the friend of the dead woman, and feels quite at ease that these letters should not have fallen into strange hands, and that they are destroyed.

Oh, how many men I know among my friends who must have burned such proofs, and who pretend to know nothing, and yet who would have fought madly had they found them when she was still alive! But she is dead. Honor has changed. The tomb is the boundary of conjugal sinning.

Therefore, I can safely keep our letters, which, in your hands, would be a menace to both of us. Do you dare to say that I am not right?

I love you and kiss you.

I raised my eyes to the portrait of Aunt Rose, and as I looked at her severe, wrinkled face, I thought of all those women's souls which we do not know, and which we suppose to be so different from what they really are, whose inborn and ingenuous craftiness we never can penetrate, their quiet duplicity; and a verse of De Vigny returned to my memory:

"Always this comrade whose heart is uncertain."

THE LOVE OF LONG AGO

The old-fashioned chateau was built on a wooded knoll in the midst of tall trees with dark-green foliage; the park extended to a great distance, in one direction to the edge of the forest, in another to the distant country. A few yards from the front of the house was a huge stone basin with marble ladies taking a bath; other, basins were seen at intervals down to the foot of the slope, and a stream of water fell in cascades from one basin to another.

From the manor house, which preserved the grace of a superannuated coquette, down to the grottos incrusted with shell-work, where slumbered the loves of a bygone age, everything in this antique demesne had retained the physiognomy of former days. Everything seemed to speak still of ancient customs, of the manners of long ago, of former gallantries, and of the elegant trivialities so dear to our grandmothers.

In a parlor in the style of Louis XV, whose walls were covered with shepherds paying court to shepherdesses, beautiful ladies in hoop-skirts, and gallant gentlemen in wigs, a very old woman, who seemed dead as soon as she ceased to move, was almost lying down in a large easy-chair, at each side of which hung a thin, mummy-like hand.

Her dim eyes were gazing dreamily toward the distant horizon as if they sought to follow through the park the visions of her youth. Through the open window every now and then came a breath of air laden with the odor of grass and the perfume of flowers. It made her white locks flutter around her wrinkled forehead and old memories float through her brain.

Beside her, on a tapestried stool, a young girl, with long fair hair hanging in braids down her back, was embroidering an altar-cloth. There was a pensive expression in her eyes, and it was easy to see that she was dreaming, while her agile fingers flew over her work.

But the old lady turned round her head, and said:

"Berthe, read me something out of the newspapers, that I may still know sometimes what is going on in the world."

The young girl took up a newspaper, and cast a rapid glance over it.

"There is a great deal about politics, grandmamma; shall I pass that over?"

"Yes, yes, darling. Are there no love stories? Is gallantry, then, dead in France, that they no longer talk about abductions or adventures as they did formerly?"

The girl made a long search through the columns of the newspaper.

"Here is one," she said. "It is entitled 'A Love Drama!'"

The old woman smiled through her wrinkles. "Read that for me," she said.

And Berthe commenced. It was a case of vitriol throwing. A wife, in order to avenge herself on her husband's mistress, had burned her face and eyes. She had left the Court of Assizes acquitted, declared to be innocent, amid the applause of the crowd.

The grandmother moved about excitedly in her chair, and exclaimed:

"This is horrible—why, it is perfectly horrible!

"See whether you can find anything else to read to me, darling."

Berthe again made a search; and farther down among the reports of criminal cases, she read:

"'Gloomy Drama. A shop girl, no longer young, allowed herself to be led astray by a young man. Then, to avenge herself on her lover, whose heart proved fickle, she shot him with a revolver. The unhappy man is maimed for life. The jury, all men of moral character, condoning the illicit love of the murderess, honorably acquitted her.'"

This time the old grandmother appeared quite shocked, and, in a trembling voice, she said:

"Why, you people are mad nowadays. You are mad! The good God has given you love, the only enchantment in life. Man has added to this gallantry the only distraction of our dull hours, and here you are mixing up with it vitriol and revolvers, as if one were to put mud into a flagon of Spanish wine."

Berthe did not seem to understand her grandmother's indignation.

"But, grandmamma, this woman avenged herself. Remember she was married, and her husband deceived her."

The grandmother gave a start.

"What ideas have they been filling your head with, you young girls of today?"

Berthe replied:

"But marriage is sacred, grandmamma."

The grandmother's heart, which had its birth in the great age of gallantry, gave a sudden leap.

"It is love that is sacred," she said. "Listen, child, to an old woman who has seen three generations, and who has had a long, long experience of men and women. Marriage and love have nothing in common. We marry to found a family, and we form families in order to constitute society. Society cannot dispense with marriage. If society is a chain, each family is a link in that chain. In order to weld those links, we always seek metals of the same order. When we marry, we must bring together suitable conditions; we must combine fortunes, unite similar races and aim at the common interest, which is riches and children. We marry only once my child, because the world requires us to do so, but we may love twenty times in one lifetime because nature has made us like this. Marriage, you see, is law, and love is an instinct which impels us, sometimes along a straight, and sometimes along a devious path. The world has made laws to combat our instincts—it was necessary to make them; but our instincts are always stronger, and we ought not to resist them too much, because they come from God; while the laws only come from men. If we did not perfume life with love, as much love as possible, darling, as we put sugar into drugs for children, nobody would care to take it just as it is."

Berthe opened her eyes wide in astonishment. She murmured:

"Oh! grandmamma, we can only love once."

The grandmother raised her trembling hands toward Heaven, as if again to invoke the defunct god of gallantries. She exclaimed indignantly:

"You have become a race of serfs, a race of common people. Since the Revolution, it is impossible any longer to recognize society. You have attached big words to every action, and wearisome duties to every corner of existence; you believe in equality and eternal passion. People have written poetry telling you that people have died of love. In my time poetry was written to teach men to love every woman. And we! when we liked a gentleman, my child, we sent him a page. And when a fresh caprice came into our hearts, we were not slow in getting rid of the last Lover—unless we kept both of them."

The old woman smiled a keen smile, and a gleam of roguery twinkled in her gray eye, the intellectual, skeptical roguery of those people who did not believe that they were made of the same clay as the rest, and who lived as masters for whom common beliefs were not intended.

The young girl, turning very pale, faltered out:

"So, then, women have no honor?"

The grandmother ceased to smile. If she had kept in her soul some of Voltaire's irony, she had also a little of Jean Jacques's glowing philosophy: "No honor! because we loved, and dared to say so, and even boasted of it? But, my child, if one of us, among the greatest ladies in France, had lived without a lover, she would have had the entire court laughing at her. Those who wished to live differently had only to enter a convent. And you imagine, perhaps, that your husbands will love but you alone, all their lives. As if, indeed, this could be the case. I tell you that marriage is a thing necessary in order that society should exist, but it is not in the nature of our race, do you understand? There is only one good thing in life, and that is love. And how you misunderstand it! how you spoil it! You treat it as something solemn like a sacrament, or something to be bought, like a dress."

The young girl caught the old woman's trembling hands in her own.

"Hold your tongue, I beg of you, grandmamma!"

And, on her knees, with tears in her eyes, she prayed to Heaven to bestow on her a great passion, one sole, eternal passion in accordance with the dream of modern poets, while the grandmother, kissing her on the forehead, quite imbued still with that charming, healthy reason with which gallant philosophers tinctured the thought of the eighteenth century, murmured:

"Take care, my poor darling! If you believe in such folly as that, you will be very unhappy."

FRIEND JOSEPH

They had been great friends all winter in Paris. As is always the case, they had lost sight of each other after leaving school, and had met again when they were old and gray-haired. One of them had married, but the other had remained in single blessedness.

M. de Meroul lived for six months in Paris and for six months in his little chateau at Tourbeville. Having married the daughter of a neighboring squire, he had lived a good and peaceful life in the indolence of a man who has nothing to do. Of a calm and quiet disposition, and not over-intelligent he used to spend his time quietly regretting the past, grieving over the customs and institutions of the day and continually repeating to his wife, who would lift her eyes, and sometimes her hands, to heaven, as a sign of energetic assent: "Good gracious! What a government!"

Madame de Meroul resembled her husband intellectually as though she had been his sister. She knew, by tradition, that one should above all respect the Pope and the King!

And she loved and respected them from the bottom of her heart, without knowing them, with a poetic fervor, with an hereditary devotion, with the tenderness of a wellborn woman. She was good to, the marrow of her bones. She had had no children, and never ceased mourning the fact.

On meeting his old friend, Joseph Mouradour, at a ball, M. de Meroul was filled with a deep and simple joy, for in their youth they had been intimate friends.

After the first exclamations of surprise at the changes which time had wrought in their bodies and countenances, they told each other about their lives since they had last met.

Joseph Mouradour, who was from the south of France, had become a government official. His manner was frank; he spoke rapidly and without restraint, giving his opinions without any tact. He was a Republican, one of those good fellows who do not believe in standing on ceremony, and who exercise an almost brutal freedom of speech.

He came to his friend's house and was immediately liked for his easy cordiality, in spite of his radical ideas. Madame de Meroul would exclaim:

"What a shame! Such a charming man!"

Monsieur de Meroul would say to his friend in a serious and confidential tone of voice; "You have no idea the harm that you are doing your country." He loved him all the same, for nothing is stronger than the ties of childhood taken up again at a riper age. Joseph Mouradour bantered the wife and the husband, calling them "my amiable snails," and sometimes he would solemnly declaim against people who were behind the times, against old prejudices and traditions.

When he was once started on his democratic eloquence, the couple, somewhat ill at ease, would keep silent from politeness and good-breeding; then the husband would try to turn the conversation into some other channel in order to avoid a clash. Joseph Mouradour was only seen in the intimacy of the family.

Summer came. The Merouls had no greater pleasure than to receive their friends at their country home at Tourbeville. It was a good, healthy pleasure, the enjoyments of good people and of country proprietors. They would meet their friends at the neighboring railroad station and would bring them back in their carriage, always on the lookout for compliments on the country, on its natural features, on the condition of the roads, on the cleanliness of the farm-houses, on the size of the cattle grazing in the fields, on everything within sight.

They would call attention to the remarkable speed with which their horse trotted, surprising for an animal that did heavy work part of the year behind a plow; and they would anxiously await the opinion of the newcomer on their family domain, sensitive to the least word, and thankful for the slightest good intention.

Joseph Mouradour was invited, and he accepted the invitation.

Husband and wife had come to the train, delighted to welcome him to their home. As soon as he saw them, Joseph Mouradour jumped from the train with a briskness which increased their satisfaction. He shook their hands, congratulated them, overwhelmed them with compliments.

All the way home he was charming, remarking on the height of the trees, the goodness of the crops and the speed of the horse.

When he stepped on the porch of the house, Monsieur de Meroul said, with a certain friendly solemnity:

"Consider yourself at home now."

Joseph Mouradour answered:

"Thanks, my friend; I expected as much. Anyhow, I never stand on ceremony with my friends. That's how I understand hospitality."

Then he went upstairs to dress as a farmer, he said, and he came back all togged out in blue linen, with a little straw hat and yellow shoes, a regular Parisian dressed for an outing. He also seemed to become more vulgar, more jovial, more familiar; having put on with his country clothes a free and easy manner which he judged suitable to the surroundings. His new manners shocked Monsieur and Madame de Meroul a little, for they always remained serious and dignified, even in the country, as though compelled by the two letters preceding their name to keep up a certain formality even in the closest intimacy.

After lunch they all went out to visit the farms, and the Parisian astounded the respectful peasants by his tone of comradeship.

In the evening the priest came to dinner, an old, fat priest, accustomed to dining there on Sundays, but who had been especially invited this day in honor of the new guest.

Joseph, on seeing him, made a wry face. Then he observed him with surprise, as though he were a creature of some peculiar race, which he had never been able to observe at close quarters. During the meal he told some rather free stories, allowable in the intimacy of the family, but which seemed to the Merouls a little out of place in the presence of a minister of the Church. He did not say, "Monsieur l'abbe," but simply, "Monsieur." He embarrassed the priest greatly by philosophical discussions about diverse superstitions current all over the world. He said: "Your God, monsieur, is of those who should be respected, but also one of those who should be discussed. Mine is called Reason; he has always been the enemy of yours."

The Merouls, distressed, tried to turn the trend of the conversation. The priest left very early.

Then the husband said, very quietly:

"Perhaps you went a little bit too far with the priest."

But Joseph immediately exclaimed:

"Well, that's pretty good! As if I would be on my guard with a shaveling! And say, do me the pleasure of not imposing him on me any more at meals. You can both make use of him as much as you wish, but don't serve him up to your friends, hang it!"

"But, my friends, think of his holy—"

Joseph Mouradour interrupted him:

"Yes, I know; they have to be treated like 'rosieres.' But let them respect my convictions, and I will respect theirs!"

That was all for that day.

As soon as Madame de Meroul entered the parlor, the next morning, she noticed in the middle of the table three newspapers which made her start the Voltaire, the Republique-Francaise and the Justice. Immediately Joseph Mouradour, still in blue, appeared on the threshold, attentively reading the Intransigeant. He cried:

"There's a great article in this by Rochefort. That fellow is a wonder!"

He read it aloud, emphasizing the parts which especially pleased him, so carried away by enthusiasm that he did not notice his friend's entrance. Monsieur de Meroul was holding in his hand the Gaulois for himself, the Clarion for his wife.

The fiery prose of the master writer who overthrew the empire, spouted with violence, sung in the southern accent, rang throughout the peaceful parsons seemed to spatter the walls and century-old furniture with a hail of bold, ironical and destructive words.

The man and the woman, one standing, the other sitting, were listening with astonishment, so shocked that they could not move.

In a burst of eloquence Mouradour finished the last paragraph, then exclaimed triumphantly:

"Well! that's pretty strong!"

Then, suddenly, he noticed the two sheets which his friend was carrying, and he, in turn, stood speechless from surprise. Quickly walking toward him he demanded angrily:

"What are you doing with those papers?"

Monsieur de Meroul answered hesitatingly:

"Why—those—those are my papers!"

"Your papers! What are you doing—making fun of me? You will do me the pleasure of reading mine; they will limber up your ideas, and as for yours—there! that's what I do with them."

And before his astonished host could stop him, he had seized the two newspapers and thrown them out of the window. Then he solemnly handed the Justice to Madame de Meroul, the Voltaire to her husband, while he sank down into an arm-chair to finish reading the Intransigeant.

The couple, through delicacy, made a pretense of reading a little, they then handed him back the Republican sheets, which they handled gingerly, as though they might be poisoned.

He laughed and declared:

"One week of this regime and I will have you converted to my ideas."

In truth, at the end of a week he ruled the house. He had closed the door against the priest, whom Madame de Meroul had to visit secretly; he had forbidden the Gaulois and the Clarion to be brought into the house, so that a servant had to go mysteriously to the post-office to get them, and as soon as he entered they would be hidden under sofa cushions; he arranged everything to suit himself—always charming, always good-natured, a jovial and all-powerful tyrant.

Other friends were expected, pious and conservative friends. The unhappy couple saw the impossibility of having them there then, and, not knowing what to do, one evening they announced to Joseph Mouradour that they would be obliged to absent themselves for a few days, on business, and they begged him to stay on alone. He did not appear disturbed, and answered:

"Very well, I don't mind! I will wait here as long as you wish. I have already said that there should be no formality between friends. You are perfectly right-go ahead and attend to your business. It will not offend me in the least; quite the contrary, it will make me feel much more completely one of the family. Go ahead, my friends, I will wait for you!"

Monsieur and Madame de Meroul left the following day.

He is still waiting for them.

THE EFFEMINATES

How often we hear people say, "He is charming, that man, but he is a girl, a regular girl." They are alluding to the effeminates, the bane of our land.

For we are all girl-like men in France—that is, fickle, fanciful, innocently treacherous, without consistency in our convictions or our will, violent and weak as women are.

But the most irritating of girl—men is assuredly the Parisian and the boulevardier, in whom the appearance of intelligence is more marked and who combines in himself all the attractions and all the faults of those charming creatures in an exaggerated degree in virtue of his masculine temperament.

Our Chamber of Deputies is full of girl-men. They form the greater number of the amiable opportunists whom one might call "The Charmers." These are they who control by soft words and deceitful promises, who know how to shake hands in such a manner as to win hearts, how to say "My dear friend" in a certain tactful way to people he knows the least, to change his mind without suspecting it, to be carried away by each new idea, to be sincere in their weathercock convictions, to let themselves be deceived as they deceive others, to forget the next morning what he affirmed the day before.

The newspapers are full of these effeminate men. That is probably where one finds the most, but it is also where they are most needed. The Journal des Debats and the Gazette de France are exceptions.

Assuredly, every good journalist must be somewhat effeminate—that is, at the command of the public, supple in following unconsciously the shades of public opinion, wavering and varying, sceptical and credulous, wicked and devout, a braggart and a true man, enthusiastic and ironical, and always convinced while believing in nothing.

Foreigners, our anti-types, as Mme. Abel called them, the stubborn English and the heavy Germans, regard us with a certain amazement mingled with contempt, and will continue to so regard us till the end of time. They consider us frivolous. It is not that, it is that we are girls. And that is why people love us in spite of our faults, why they come back to us despite the evil spoken of us; these are lovers' quarrels! The effeminate man, as one meets him in this world, is so charming that he captivates you after five minutes' chat. His smile seems made for you; one cannot believe that his voice does not assume specially tender intonations on their account. When he leaves you it seems as if one had known him for twenty years. One is quite ready to lend him money if he asks for it. He has enchanted you, like a woman.

If he commits any breach of manners towards you, you cannot bear any malice, he is so pleasant when you next meet him. If he asks your pardon you long to ask pardon of him. Does he tell lies? You cannot believe it. Does he put you off indefinitely with promises that he does not keep? One lays as much store by his promises as though he had moved heaven and earth to render them a service.

When he admires anything he goes into such raptures that he convinces you. He once adored Victor Hugo, whom he now treats as a back number. He would have fought for Zola, whom he has abandoned for Barbey and d'Aurevilly. And when he admires, he permits no limitation, he would slap your face for a word. But when he becomes scornful, his contempt is unbounded and allows of no protest.

In fact, he understands nothing.

Listen to two girls talking.

"Then you are angry with Julia?" "I slapped her face." "What had she done?" "She told Pauline that I had no money thirteen months out of twelve, and Pauline told Gontran—you understand." "You were living together in the Rue Clanzel?" "We lived together four years in the Rue Breda; we quarrelled about a pair of stockings that she said I had worn —it wasn't true—silk stockings that she had bought at Mother Martin's. Then I gave her a pounding and she left me at once. I met her six months ago and she asked me to come and live with her, as she has rented a flat that is twice too large."

One goes on one's way and hears no more. But on the following Sunday as one is on the way to Saint Germain two young women get into the same railway carriage. One recognizes one of them at once; it is Julia's enemy. The other is Julia!

And there are endearments, caresses, plans. "Say, Julia—listen, Julia," etc.

The girl-man has his friendships of this kind. For three months he cannot bear to leave his old Jack, his dear Jack. There is no one but Jack in the world. He is the only one who has any intelligence, any sense, any talent. He alone amounts to anything in Paris. One meets them everywhere together, they dine together, walk about in company, and every evening walk home with each other back and forth without being able to part with one another.

Three months later, if Jack is mentioned:

"There is a drinker, a sorry fellow, a scoundrel for you. I know him well, you may be sure. And he is not even honest, and ill-bred," etc., etc.

Three months later, and they are living together.

But one morning one hears that they have fought a duel, then embraced each other, amid tears, on the duelling ground.

Just now they are the dearest friends in the world, furious with each other half the year, abusing and loving each other by turns, squeezing each other's hands till they almost crush the bones, and ready to run each other through the body for a misunderstanding.

For the relations of these effeminate men are uncertain. Their temper is by fits and starts, their delight unexpected, their affection turn-about-face, their enthusiasm subject to eclipse. One day they love you, the next day they will hardly look at you, for they have in fact a girl's nature, a girl's charm, a girl's temperament, and all their sentiments are like the affections of girls.

They treat their friends as women treat their pet dogs.

It is the dear little Toutou whom they hug, feed with sugar, allow to sleep on the pillow, but whom they would be just as likely to throw out of a window in a moment of impatience, whom they turn round like a sling, holding it by the tail, squeeze in their arms till they almost strangle it, and plunge, without any reason, in a pail of cold water.

Then, what a strange thing it is when one of these beings falls in love with a real girl! He beats her, she scratches him, they execrate each other, cannot bear the sight of each other and yet cannot part, linked together by no one knows what mysterious psychic bonds. She deceives him, he knows it, sobs and forgives her. He despises and adores her without seeing that she would be justified in despising him. They are both atrociously unhappy and yet cannot separate. They cast invectives, reproaches and abominable accusations at each other from morning till night, and when they have reached the climax and are vibrating with rage and hatred, they fall into each other's arms and kiss each other ardently.

The girl-man is brave and a coward at the same time. He has, more than another, the exalted sentiment of honor, but is lacking in the sense of simple honesty, and, circumstances favoring him, would defalcate and commit infamies which do not trouble his conscience, for he obeys without questioning the oscillations of his ideas, which are always impulsive.

To him it seems permissible and almost right to cheat a haberdasher. He considers it honorable not to pay his debts, unless they are gambling debts—that is, somewhat shady. He dupes people whenever the laws of society admit of his doing so. When he is short of money he borrows in all ways, not always being scrupulous as to tricking the lenders, but he would, with sincere indignation, run his sword through anyone who should suspect him of only lacking in politeness.

OLD AMABLE

PART I

The humid gray sky seemed to weigh down on the vast brown plain. The odor of autumn, the sad odor of bare, moist lands, of fallen leaves, of dead grass made the stagnant evening air more thick and heavy. The peasants were still at work, scattered through the fields, waiting for the stroke of the Angelus to call them back to the farmhouses, whose thatched roofs were visible here and there through the branches of the leafless trees which protected the apple-gardens against the wind.

At the side of the road, on a heap of clothes, a very small boy seated with his legs apart was playing with a potato, which he now and then let fall on his dress, whilst five women were bending down planting slips of colza in the adjoining plain. With a slow, continuous movement, all along the mounds of earth which the plough had just turned up, they drove in sharp wooden stakes and in the hole thus formed placed the plant, already a little withered, which sank on one side; then they patted down the earth and went on with their work.

A man who was passing, with a whip in his hand, and wearing wooden shoes, stopped near the child, took it up and kissed it. Then one of the women rose up and came across to him. She was a big, red haired girl, with large hips, waist and shoulders, a tall Norman woman, with yellow hair in which there was a blood-red tint.

She said in a resolute voice:

"Why, here you are, Cesaire—well?"

The man, a thin young fellow with a melancholy air, murmured:

"Well, nothing at all—always the same thing."

"He won't have it?"

"He won't have it."

"What are you going to do?"

"What do you say I ought to do?"

"Go see the cure."

"I will."

"Go at once!"

"I will."

And they stared at each other. He held the child in his arms all the time. He kissed it once more and then put it down again on the woman's clothes.

In the distance, between two farm-houses, could be seen a plough drawn by a horse and driven by a man. They moved on very gently, the horse, the plough and the laborer, in the dim evening twilight.

The woman went on:

"What did your father say?"

"He said he would not have it."

"Why wouldn't he have it?"

The young man pointed toward the child whom he had just put back on the ground, then with a glance he drew her attention to the man drawing the plough yonder there.

And he said emphatically:

"Because 'tis his—this child of yours."

The girl shrugged her shoulders and in an angry tone said:

"Faith, every one knows it well—that it is Victor's. And what about it after all? I made a slip. Am I the only woman that did? My mother also made a slip before me, and then yours did the same before she married your dad! Who is it that hasn't made a slip in the country? I made a slip with Victor because he took advantage of me while I was asleep in the barn, it's true, and afterward it happened between us when I wasn't asleep. I certainly would have married him if he weren't a servant man. Am I a worse woman for that?"

The man said simply:

"As for me, I like you just as you are, with or without the child. It's only my father that opposes me. All the same, I'll see about settling the business."

She answered:

"Go to the cure at once."

"I'm going to him."

And he set forth with his heavy peasant's tread, while the girl, with her hands on her hips, turned round to plant her colza.

In fact, the man who thus went off, Cesaire Houlbreque, the son of deaf old Amable Houlbreque, wanted to marry, in spite of his father, Celeste Levesque, who had a child by Victor Lecoq, a mere laborer on her parents' farm, who had been turned out of doors for this act.

The hierarchy of caste, however, does not exist in the country, and if the laborer is thrifty, he becomes, by taking a farm in his turn, the equal of his former master.

So Cesaire Houlbieque went off, his whip under his arm, brooding over his own thoughts and lifting up one after the other his heavy wooden shoes daubed with clay. Certainly he desired to marry Celeste Levesque. He wanted her with her child because she was the wife he wanted. He could not say why, but he knew it, he was sure of it. He had only to look at her to be convinced of it, to feel quite queer, quite stirred up, simply stupid with happiness. He even found a pleasure in kissing the little boy, Victor's little boy, because he belonged to her.

And he gazed, without hate, at the distant outline of the man who was driving his plough along the horizon.

But old Amable did not want this marriage. He opposed it with the obstinacy of a deaf man, with a violent obstinacy.

Cesaire in vain shouted in his ear, in that ear which still heard a few sounds:

"I'll take good care of you, daddy. I tell you she's a good girl and strong, too, and also thrifty."

The old man repeated:

"As long as I live I won't see her your wife."

And nothing could get the better of him, nothing could make him waver. One hope only was left to Cesaire. Old Amable was afraid of the cure through the apprehension of death which he felt drawing nigh; he had not much fear of God, nor of the Devil, nor of Hell, nor of Purgatory, of which he had no conception, but he dreaded the priest, who represented to him burial, as one might fear the doctors through horror of diseases. For the last tight days Celeste, who knew this weakness of the old man, had been urging Cesaire to go and find the cure, but Cesaire always hesitated, because he had not much liking for the black robe, which represented to him hands always stretched out for collections or for blessed bread.

However, he had made up his mind, and he proceeded toward the presbytery, thinking in what manner he would speak about his case.

The Abbe Raffin, a lively little priest, thin and never shaved, was awaiting his dinner-hour while warming his feet at his kitchen fire.

As soon as he saw the peasant entering he asked, merely turning his head:

"Well, Cesaire, what do you want?"

"I'd like to have a talk with you, M. le Cure."

The man remained standing, intimidated, holding his cap in one hand and his whip in the other.

"Well, talk."

Cesaire looked at the housekeeper, an old woman who dragged her feet while putting on the cover for her master's dinner at the corner of the table in front of the window.

He stammered:

"'Tis—'tis a sort of confession."

Thereupon the Abbe Raffin carefully surveyed his peasant. He saw his confused countenance, his air of constraint, his wandering eyes, and he gave orders to the housekeeper in these words:

"Marie, go away for five minutes to your room, while I talk to Cesaire."

The servant cast on the man an angry glance and went away grumbling.

The clergyman went on:

"Come, now, tell your story."

The young fellow still hesitated, looked down at his wooden shoes, moved about his cap, then, all of a sudden, he made up his mind:

"Here it is: I want to marry Celeste Levesque."

"Well, my boy, what's there to prevent you?"

"The father won't have it."

"Your father?"

"Yes, my father."

"What does your father say?"

"He says she has a child."

"She's not the first to whom that happened, since our Mother Eve."

"A child by Victor Lecoq, Anthime Loisel's servant man."

"Ha! ha! So he won't have it?"

"He won't have it."

"What! not at all?"

"No, no more than an ass that won't budge an inch, saving your presence."

"What do you say to him yourself in order to make him decide?"

"I say to him that she's a good girl, and strong, too, and thrifty also."

"And this does not make him agree to it. So you want me to speak to him?"

"Exactly. You speak to him."

"And what am I to tell your father?"

"Why, what you tell people in your sermons to make them give you sous."

In the peasant's mind every effort of religion consisted in loosening the purse strings, in emptying the pockets of men in order to fill the heavenly coffer. It was a kind of huge commercial establishment, of which the cures were the clerks; sly, crafty clerks, sharp as any one must be who does business for the good God at the expense of the country people.

He knew full well that the priests rendered services, great services to the poorest, to the sick and dying, that they assisted, consoled, counselled, sustained, but all this by means of money, in exchange for white pieces, for beautiful glittering coins, with which they paid for sacraments and masses, advice and protection, pardon of sins and indulgences, purgatory and paradise according to the yearly income and the generosity of the sinner.

The Abbe Raffin, who knew his man and who never lost his temper, burst out laughing.

"Well, yes, I'll tell your father my little story; but you, my lad, you'll come to church."

Houlbreque extended his hand in order to give a solemn assurance:

"On the word of a poor man, if you do this for me, I promise that I will."

"Come, that's all right. When do you wish me to go and find your father?"

"Why, the sooner the better-to-night, if you can."

"In half an hour, then, after supper."

"In half an hour."

"That's understood. So long, my lad."

"Good-by till we meet again, Monsieur le Cure; many thanks."

"Not at all, my lad."

And Cesaire Houlbreque returned home, his heart relieved of a great weight.

He held on lease a little farm, quite small, for they were not rich, his father and he. Alone with a female servant, a little girl of fifteen, who made the soup, looked after the fowls, milked the cows and churned the butter, they lived frugally, though Cesaire was a good cultivator. But they did not possess either sufficient lands or sufficient cattle to earn more than the indispensable.

The old man no longer worked. Sad, like all deaf people, crippled with pains, bent double, twisted, he went through the fields leaning on his stick, watching the animals and the men with a hard, distrustful eye. Sometimes he sat down on the side of the road and remained there without moving for hours, vaguely pondering over the things that had engrossed his whole life, the price of eggs, and corn, the sun and the rain which spoil the crops or make them grow. And, worn out with rheumatism, his old limbs still drank in the humidity of the soul, as they had drunk in for the past sixty years, the moisture of the walls of his low house thatched with damp straw.

He came back at the close of the day, took his place at the end of the table in the kitchen and when the earthen bowl containing the soup had been placed before him he placed round it his crooked fingers, which seemed to have kept the round form of the bowl and, winter and summer, he warmed his hands, before commencing to eat, so as to lose nothing, not even a particle of the heat that came from the fire, which costs a great deal, neither one drop of soup into which fat and salt have to be put, nor one morsel of bread, which comes from the wheat.

Then he climbed up a ladder into a loft, where he had his strawbed, while his son slept below stairs at the end of a kind of niche near the chimneypiece and the servant shut herself up in a kind of cellar, a black hole which was formerly used to store the potatoes.

Cesaire and his father scarcely ever talked to each other. From time to time only, when there was a question of selling a crop or buying a calf, the young man would ask his father's advice, and, making a speaking-trumpet of his two hands, he would bawl out his views into his ear, and old Amable either approved of them or opposed them in a slow, hollow voice that came from the depths of his stomach.

So one evening Cesaire, approaching him as if about to discuss the purchase of a horse or a heifer, communicated to him at the top of his voice his intention to marry Celeste Levesque.

Then the father got angry. Why? On the score of morality? No, certainly. The virtue of a girl is of slight importance in the country. But his avarice, his deep, fierce instinct for saving, revolted at the idea that his son should bring up a child which he had not begotten himself. He had thought suddenly, in one second, of the soup the little fellow would swallow before becoming useful on the farm. He had calculated all the pounds of bread, all the pints of cider that this brat would consume up to his fourteenth year, and a mad anger broke loose from him against Cesaire, who had not bestowed a thought on all this.

He replied in an unusually strong voice:

"Have you lost your senses?"

Thereupon Cesaire began to enumerate his reasons, to speak

about Celeste's good qualities, to prove that she would be worth a thousand times what the child would cost. But the old man doubted these advantages, while he could have no doubts as to the child's existence; and he replied with emphatic repetition, without giving any further explanation:

"I will not have it! I will not have it! As long as I live, this won't be done!" And at this point they had remained for the last three months without one or the other giving in, resuming at least once a week the same discussion, with the same arguments, the same words, the same gestures and the same fruitlessness.

It was then that Celeste had advised Cesaire to go and ask for the cure's assistance.

On arriving home the peasant found his father already seated at table, for he came late through his visit to the presbytery.

They dined in silence, face to face, ate a little bread and butter after the soup and drank a glass of cider. Then they remained motionless in their chairs, with scarcely a glimmer of light, the little servant girl having carried off the candle in order to wash the spoons, wipe the glasses and cut the crusts of bread to be ready for next morning's breakfast.

There was a knock, at the door, which was immediately opened, and the priest appeared. The old man raised toward him an anxious eye full of suspicion, and, foreseeing danger, he was getting ready to climb up his ladder when the Abbe Raffin laid his hand on his shoulder and shouted close to his temple:

"I want to have a talk with you, Father Amable."

Cesaire had disappeared, taking advantage of the door being open. He did not want to listen, for he was afraid and did not want his hopes to crumble slowly with each obstinate refusal of his father. He preferred to learn the truth at once, good or bad, later on; and he went out into the night. It was a moonless, starless night, one of those misty nights when the air seems thick with humidity. A vague odor of apples floated through the farmyard, for it was the season when the earliest applies were gathered, the "early ripe," as they are called in the cider country. As Cesaire passed along by the cattlesheds the warm smell of living beasts asleep on manure was exhaled through the narrow windows, and he heard the stamping of the horses, who were standing at the end of the stable, and the sound of their jaws tearing and munching the hay on the racks.

He went straight ahead, thinking about Celeste. In this simple nature, whose ideas were scarcely more than images generated directly by objects, thoughts of love only formulated themselves by calling up before the mind the picture of a big red-haired girl standing in a hollow road and laughing, with her hands on her hips.

It was thus he saw her on the day when he first took a fancy for her. He had, however, known her from infancy, but never had he been so struck by her as on that morning. They had stopped to talk for a few minutes and then he went away, and as he walked along he kept repeating:

"Faith, she's a fine girl, all the same. 'Tis a pity she made a slip with Victor."

Till evening he kept thinking of her and also on the following morning.

When he saw her again he felt something tickling the end of his throat, as if a cock's feather had been driven through his mouth into his chest, and since then, every time he found himself near her, he was astonished at this nervous tickling which always commenced again.

In three months he made up his mind to marry her, so much did she please him. He could not have said whence came this power over him, but he explained it in these words:

"I am possessed by her," as if the desire for this girl within him were as dominating as one of the powers of hell. He scarcely bothered himself about her transgression. It was a pity, but, after all, it did her no harm, and he bore no grudge against Victor Lecoq.

But if the cure should not succeed, what was he to do? He did not dare to think of it, the anxiety was such a torture to him.

He reached the presbytery and seated himself near the little gateway to wait for the priest's return.

He was there perhaps half an hour when he heard steps on the road, and although the night was very dark, he presently distinguished the still darker shadow of the cassock.

He rose up, his legs giving way under him, not even venturing to speak, not daring to ask a question.

The clergyman perceived him and said gaily:

"Well, my lad, it's all right."

Cesaire stammered:

"All right, 'tisn't possible."

"Yes, my lad, but not without trouble. What an old ass your father is!"

The peasant repeated:

"'Tisn't possible!"

"Why, yes. Come and look me up to-morrow at midday in order to settle about the publication of the banns."

The young man seized the cure's hand. He pressed it, shook it, bruised it as he stammered:

"True-true-true, Monsieur le Cure, on the word of an honest man, you'll see me to-morrow-at your sermon."

PART II

The wedding took place in the middle of December. It was simple, the bridal pair not being rich. Cesaire, attired in new clothes, was ready since eight o'clock in the morning to go and fetch his betrothed and bring her to the mayor's office, but it was too early. He seated himself before the kitchen table and waited for the members of the family and the friends who were to accompany him.

For the last eight days it had been snowing, and the brown earth, the earth already fertilized by the autumn sowing, had become a dead white, sleeping under a great sheet of ice.

It was cold in the thatched houses adorned with white caps, and the round apples in the trees of the enclosures seemed to be flowering, covered with white as they had been in the pleasant month of their blossoming.

This day the big clouds to the north, the big great snow clouds, had disappeared and the blue sky showed itself above the white earth on which the rising sun cast silvery reflections.

Cesaire looked straight before him through the window, thinking of nothing, quite happy.

The door opened, two women entered, peasant women in their Sunday clothes, the aunt and the cousin of the bridegroom; then three men, his cousins; then a woman who was a neighbor. They sat down on chairs and remained, motionless and silent, the women on one side of the kitchen, the men on the other, suddenly seized with timidity, with that embarrassed sadness which takes possession of people assembled for a ceremony. One of the cousins soon asked:

"Is it not the hour?"

Cesaire replied:

"I am much afraid it is."

"Come on! Let us start," said another.

Those rose up. Then Cesaire, whom a feeling of uneasiness had taken possession of, climbed up the ladder of the loft to see whether his father was ready. The old man, always as a rule an early riser, had not yet made his appearance. His son found him on his bed of straw, wrapped up in his blanket, with his eyes open and a malicious gleam in them.

He bawled into his ear: "Come, daddy, get up. It's time for the wedding."

The deaf man murmured-in a doleful tone:

"I can't get up. I have a sort of chill over me that freezes my back. I can't stir."

The young man, dumbfounded, stared at him, guessing that this was a dodge.

"Come, daddy; you must make an effort."

"I can't do it."

"Look here! I'll help you."

And he stooped toward the old man, pulled off his blanket, caught him by the arm and lifted him up. But old Amable began to whine, "Ooh! ooh! ooh! What suffering! Ooh! I can't. My back is stiffened up. The cold wind must have rushed in through this cursed roof."

"Well, you'll get no dinner, as I'm having a spread at Polyte's inn. This will teach you what comes of acting mulishly."

And he hurried down the ladder and started out, accompanied by his relatives and guests.

The men had turned up the bottoms of their trousers so as not to get them wet in the snow. The women held up their petticoats and showed their lean ankles with gray woollen stockings and their bony shanks resembling broomsticks. And they all moved forward with a swinging gait, one behind the other, without uttering a word, moving cautiously, for fear of losing the road which was-hidden beneath the flat, uniform, uninterrupted stretch of snow.

As they approached the farmhouses they saw one or two persons waiting to join them, and the procession went on without stopping and wound its way forward, following the invisible outlines of the road, so that it resembled a living chaplet of black beads undulating through the white countryside.

In front of the bride's door a large group was stamping up and down the open space awaiting the bridegroom. When he appeared they gave him a loud greeting, and presently Celeste came forth from her room, clad in a blue dress, her shoulders covered with a small red shawl and her head adorned with orange flowers.

But every one asked Cesaire:

"Where's your father?"

He replied with embarrassment:

"He couldn't move on account of the pains."

And the farmers tossed their heads with a sly, incredulous air.

They directed their steps toward the mayor's office. Behind the pair about to be wedded a peasant woman carried Victor's child, as if it were going to be baptized; and the peasants, in pairs now, with arms linked, walked through the snow with the movements of a sloop at sea.

After having been united by the mayor in the little municipal house the pair were made one by the cure, in his turn, in the modest house of God. He blessed their union by promising them fruitfulness, then he preached to them on the matrimonial virtues, the simple and healthful virtues of the country, work, concord and fidelity, while the child, who was cold, began to fret behind the bride.

As soon as the couple reappeared on the threshold of the church shots were discharged from the ditch of the cemetery. Only the barrels of the guns could be seen whence came forth rapid jets of smoke; then a head could be seen gazing at the procession. It was Victor Lecoq celebrating the marriage of his old sweetheart, wishing her happiness and sending her his good wishes with explosions of powder. He had employed some friends of his, five or six laboring men, for these salvos of musketry. It was considered a nice attention.

The repast was given in Polyte Cacheprune's inn. Twenty covers were laid in the great hall where people dined on market days, and the big leg of mutton turning before the spit, the fowls browned under their own gravy, the chitterlings sputtering over the bright, clear fire filled the house with a thick odor of live coal sprinkled with fat—the powerful, heavy odor of rustic fare.

They sat down to table at midday and the soup was poured at once into the plates. All faces had already brightened up; mouths opened to utter loud jokes and eyes were laughing with knowing winks. They were going to amuse themselves and no mistake.

The door opened, and old Amable appeared. He seemed in a bad humor and his face wore a scowl as he dragged himself forward on his sticks, whining at every step to indicate his suffering. As soon as they saw him they stopped talking, but suddenly his neighbor, Daddy Malivoire, a big joker, who knew all the little tricks and ways of people, began to yell, just as Cesaire used to do, by making a speaking-trumpet of his hands.

"Hallo, my cute old boy, you have a good nose on you to be able to smell Polyte's cookery from your own house!"

A roar of laughter burst forth from the throats of those present. Malivoire, excited by his success, went on:

"There's nothing for the rheumatics like a chitterling poultice! It keeps your belly warm, along with a glass of three-six!"

The men uttered shouts, banged the table with their fists, laughed, bending on one side and raising up their bodies again as if they were working a pump. The women clucked like hens, while the servants wriggled, standing against the walls. Old Amable was the only one that did not laugh, and, without making any reply, waited till they made room for him.

They found a place for him in the middle of the table, facing his daughter-in-law, and, as soon as he was seated, he began to eat. It was his son who was paying, after all; it was right he should take his share. With each ladleful of soup that went into his stomach, with each mouthful of bread or meat crushed between his gums, with each glass of cider or wine that flowed through his gullet he thought he was regaining something of his own property, getting back a little of his money which all those gluttons were devouring, saving in fact a portion of his own means. And he ate in silence with the obstinacy of a miser who hides his coppers, with the same gloomy persistence with which he formerly performed his daily labors.

But all of a sudden he noticed at the end of the table Celeste's child on a woman's lap, and his eye remained fixed on the little boy. He went on eating, with his glance riveted on the youngster, into whose mouth the woman who minded him every now and then put a little morsel which he nibbled at. And the old man suffered more from the few mouthfuls sucked by this little chap than from all that the others swallowed.

The meal lasted till evening. Then every one went back home.

Cesaire raised up old Amable.

"Come, daddy, we must go home," said he.

And he put the old man's two sticks in his hands.

Celeste took her child in her arms, and they went on slowly through the pale night whitened by the snow. The deaf old man, three-fourths tipsy, and even more malicious under the influence of drink, refused to go forward. Several times he even sat down with the object of making his daughter-in-law catch cold, and he kept whining, without uttering a word, giving vent to a sort of continuous groaning as if he were in pain.

When they reached home he at once climbed up to his loft, while Cesaire made a bed for the child near the deep niche where he was going to lie down with his wife. But as the newly wedded pair could not sleep immediately, they heard the old man for a long time moving about on his bed of straw, and he even talked aloud several times, whether it was that he was dreaming or that he let his thoughts escape through his mouth, in spite of himself, not being able to keep them back, under the obsession of a fixed idea.

When he came down his ladder next morning he saw his daughter-in-law looking after the housekeeping.

She cried out to him:

"Come, daddy, hurry on! Here's some good soup."

And she placed at the end of the table the round black earthen bowl filled with steaming liquid. He sat down without giving any answer, seized the hot bowl, warmed his hands with it in his customary fashion, and, as it was very cold, even pressed it against his breast to try to make a little of the living heat of the boiling liquid enter into him, into his old body stiffened by so many winters.

Then he took his sticks and went out into the fields, covered with ice, till it was time for dinner, for he had seen Celeste's youngster still asleep in a big soap-box.

He did not take his place in the household. He lived in the thatched house, as in bygone days, but he seemed not to belong to it any longer, to be no longer interested in anything, to look upon those people, his son, the wife and the child as strangers whom he did not know, to whom he never spoke.

The winter glided by. It was long and severe.

Then the early spring made the seeds sprout forth again, and the peasants once more, like laborious ants, passed their days in the fields, toiling from morning till night, under the wind and under the rain, along the furrows of brown earth which brought forth the bread of men.

The year promised well for the newly married pair. The crops grew thick and strong. There were no late frosts, and the apples bursting into bloom scattered on the grass their rosy white snow which promised a hail of fruit for the autumn.

Cesaire toiled hard, rose early and left off work late, in order to save the expense of a hired man.

His wife said to him sometimes:

"You'll make yourself ill in the long run."

He replied:

"Certainly not. I'm a good judge."

Nevertheless one evening he came home so fatigued that he had to get to bed without supper. He rose up next morning at the usual hour, but he could not eat, in spite of his fast on the previous night, and he had to come back to the house in the middle of the afternoon in order to go to bed again. In the course of the night he began to cough; he turned round on his straw couch, feverish, with his forehead burning, his tongue dry and his throat parched by a burning thirst.

However, at daybreak he went toward his grounds, but next morning the doctor had to be sent for and pronounced him very ill with inflammation of the lungs.

And he no longer left the dark recess in which he slept. He could be heard coughing, gasping and tossing about in this hole. In order to see him, to give his medicine and to apply cupping-glasses they had to bring a candle to the entrance. Then one could see his narrow head with his long matted beard underneath a thick lacework of spiders' webs, which hung and floated when stirred by the air. And the hands of the sick man seemed dead under the dingy sheets.

Celeste watched him with restless activity, made him take physic, applied blisters to him, went back and forth in the house, while old Amable remained at the edge of his loft, watching at a distance the gloomy cavern where his son lay dying. He did not come near him, through hatred of the wife, sulking like an ill-tempered dog.

Six more days passed, then one morning, as Celeste, who now slept on the ground on two loose bundles of straw, was going to see whether her man was better, she no longer heard his rapid breathing from the interior of his recess. Terror stricken, she asked:

"Well Cesaire, what sort of a night had you?"

He did not answer. She put out her hand to touch him, and the flesh on his face felt cold as ice. She uttered a great cry, the long cry of a woman overpowered with fright. He was dead.

At this cry the deaf old man appeared at the top of his ladder, and when he saw Celeste rushing to call for help, he quickly descended, placed his hand on his son's face, and suddenly realizing what had happened, went to shut the door from the inside, to prevent the wife from re-entering and resuming possession of the dwelling, since his son was no longer living.

Then he sat down on a chair by the dead man's side.

Some of the neighbors arrived, called out and knocked. He did not hear them. One of them broke the glass of the window and jumped into the room. Others followed. The door was opened again and Celeste reappeared, all in tears, with swollen face and bloodshot eyes. Then old Amable, vanquished, without uttering a word, climbed back to his loft.

The funeral took place next morning. Then, after the ceremony, the father-in-law and the daughter-in-law found themselves alone in the farmhouse with the child.

It was the usual dinner hour. She lighted the fire, made some soup and placed the plates on the table, while the old man sat on the chair waiting without appearing to look at her. When the meal was ready she bawled in his ear—

"Come, daddy, you must eat." He rose up, took his seat at the end of the table, emptied his soup bowl, masticated his bread and butter, drank his two glasses of cider and then took himself off.

It was one of those warm days, one of those enjoyable days when life ferments, pulsates, blooms all over the surface of the soil.

Old Amable pursued a little path across the fields. He looked at the young wheat and the young oats, thinking that his son was now under the earth, his poor boy! He walked along wearily, dragging his legs after him in a limping fashion. And, as he was all alone in the plain, all alone under the blue sky, in the midst of the growing crops, all alone with the larks which he saw hovering above his head, without hearing their light song, he began to weep as he proceeded on his way.

Then he sat down beside a pond and remained there till evening, gazing at the little birds that came there to drink. Then, as the night was falling, he returned to the house, supped without saying a word and climbed up to his loft. And his life went on as in the past. Nothing was changed, except that his son Cesaire slept in the cemetery.

What could he, an old man, do? He could work no longer; he was now good for nothing except to swallow the soup prepared by his daughter-in-law. And he ate it in silence, morning and evening, watching with an eye of rage the little boy also taking soup, right opposite him, at the other side of the table. Then he would go out, prowl about the fields after the fashion of a vagabond, hiding behind the barns where he would sleep for an hour or two as if he were afraid of being seen and then come back at the approach of night.

But Celeste's mind began to be occupied by graver anxieties. The farm needed a man to look after it and cultivate it. Somebody should be there always to go through the fields, not a mere hired laborer, but a regular farmer, a master who understood the business and would take an interest in the farm. A lone woman could not manage the farming, watch the price of corn and direct the sale and purchase of cattle. Then ideas came into her head, simple practical ideas, which she had turned over in her head at night. She could not marry again before the end of the year, and it was necessary at once to take care of pressing interests, immediate interests.

Only one man could help her out of her difficulties, Victor Lecoq, the father of her child. He was strong and understood farming; with a little money in his pocket he would make an excellent cultivator. She was aware of his skill, having known him while he was working on her parents' farm.

So one morning, seeing him passing along the road with a cart of manure, she went out to meet him. When he perceived her, he drew up his horses and she said to him as if she had met him the night before:

"Good-morrow, Victor—are you quite well, the same as ever?"

He replied:

"I'm quite well, the same as ever—and how are you?"

"Oh, I'd be all right, only that I'm alone in the house, which bothers me on account of the farm."

Then they remained chatting for a long time, leaning against the wheel of the heavy cart. The man every now and then lifted up his cap to scratch his forehead and began thinking, while she, with flushed cheeks, went on talking warmly, told him about her views, her plans; her projects for the future. At last he said in a low tone:

"Yes, it can be done."

She opened her hand like a countryman clinching a bargain and asked:

"Is it agreed?"

He pressed her outstretched hand.

"'Tis agreed."

"It's settled, then, for next Sunday?"

"It's settled for next Sunday"

"Well, good-morning, Victor."

"Good-morning, Madame Houlbreque."

PART III

This particular Sunday was the day of the village festival, the annual festival in honor of the patron saint, which in Normandy is called the assembly.

For the last eight days quaint-looking vehicles in which live the families of strolling fair exhibitors, lottery managers, keepers of shooting galleries and other forms of amusement or exhibitors of curiosities whom the peasants call "wonder-makers" could be seen coming along the roads drawn slowly by gray or sorrel horses.

The dirty wagons with their floating curtains, accompanied by a melancholy-looking dog, who trotted, with his head down, between the wheels, drew up one after the other on the green in front of the town hall. Then a tent was erected in front of each ambulant abode, and inside this tent could be seen, through the holes in the canvas, glittering things which excited the envy or the curiosity of the village youngsters.

As soon as the morning of the fete arrived all the booths were opened, displaying their splendors of glass or porcelain, and the peasants on their way to mass looked with genuine satisfaction at these modest shops which they saw again, nevertheless, each succeeding year.

Early in the afternoon there was a crowd on the green. From every neighboring village the farmers arrived, shaken along with their wives and children in the two-wheeled open chars-a-bancs, which rattled along, swaying like cradles. They unharnessed at their friends' houses and the farmyards were filled with strange-looking traps, gray, high, lean, crooked, like long-clawed creatures from the depths of the sea. And each family, with the youngsters in front and the grown-up ones behind, came to the assembly with tranquil steps, smiling countenances and open hands, big hands, red and bony, accustomed to work and apparently tired of their temporary rest.

A clown was blowing a trumpet. The barrel-organ accompanying the carrousel sent through the air its shrill jerky notes. The lottery-wheel made a whirring sound like that of cloth tearing, and every moment the crack of the rifle could be heard. And the slow-moving throng passed on quietly in front of the booths resembling paste in a fluid condition, with the motions of a flock of sheep and the awkwardness of heavy animals who had escaped by chance.

The girls, holding one another's arms in groups of six or eight, were singing; the youths followed them, making jokes, with their caps over their ears and their blouses stiffened with starch, swollen out like blue balloons.

The whole countryside was there—masters, laboring men and women servants.

Old Amable himself, wearing his old-fashioned green frock coat, had wished to see the assembly, for he never failed to attend on such an occasion.

He looked at the lotteries, stopped in front of the shooting galleries to criticize the shots and interested himself specially in a very simple game which consisted in throwing a big wooden ball into the open mouth of a mannikin carved and painted on a board.

Suddenly he felt a tap on his shoulder. It was Daddy Malivoire, who exclaimed:

"Ha, daddy! Come and have a glass of brandy."

And they sat down at the table of an open-air restaurant.

They drank one glass of brandy, then two, then three, and old Amable once more began wandering through the assembly. His thoughts became slightly confused, he smiled without knowing why, he smiled in front of the lotteries, in front of the wooden horses and especially in front of the killing game. He remained there a long time, filled with delight, when he saw a holiday-maker knocking down the gendarme or the cure, two authorities whom he instinctively distrusted. Then he went back to the inn and drank a glass of cider to cool himself. It was late, night came on. A neighbor came to warn him:

"You'll get back home late for the stew, daddy."

Then he set out on his way to the farmhouse. A soft shadow, the warm shadow of a spring night, was slowly descending on the earth.

When he reached the front door he thought he saw through the window which was lighted up two persons in the house. He stopped, much surprised, then he went in, and he saw Victor Lecoq seated at the table, with a plate filled with potatoes before him, taking his supper in the very same place where his son had sat.

And he turned round suddenly as if he wanted to go away. The night was very dark now. Celeste started up and shouted at him:

"Come quick, daddy! Here's some good stew to finish off the assembly with."

He complied through inertia and sat down, watching in turn the man, the woman and the child. Then he began to eat quietly as on ordinary days.

Victor Lecoq seemed quite at home, talked from time to time to Celeste, took up the child in his lap and kissed him. And Celeste again served him with food, poured out drink for him and appeared happy while speaking to him. Old Amable's eyes followed them attentively, though he could not hear what they were saying.

When he had finished supper (and he had scarcely eaten anything, there was such a weight at his heart) he rose up, and instead of ascending to his loft as he did every night he opened the gate of the yard and went out into the open air.

When he had gone, Celeste, a little uneasy, asked:

"What is he going to do?"

Victor replied in an indifferent tone:

128

"Don't bother yourself. He'll come back when he's tired."

Then she saw after the house, washed the plates and wiped the table, while the man quietly took off his clothes. Then he slipped into the dark and hollow bed in which she had slept with Cesaire.

The yard gate opened and old Amable again appeared. As soon as he entered the house he looked round on every side with the air of an old dog on the scent. He was in search of Victor Lecoq. As he did not see him, he took the candle off the table and approached the dark niche in which his son had died. In the interior of it he perceived the man lying under the bed clothes and already asleep. Then the deaf man noiselessly turned round, put back the candle and went out into the yard.

Celeste had finished her work. She put her son into his bed, arranged everything and waited for her father-in-law's return before lying down herself.

She remained sitting on a chair, without moving her hands and with her eyes fixed on vacancy.

As he did not come back, she murmured in a tone of impatience and annoyance:

"This good-for-nothing old man will make us burn four sous' worth of candles."

Victor answered from under the bed clothes:

"It's over an hour since he went out. We ought to see whether he fell asleep on the bench outside the door."

"I'll go and see," she said.

She rose up, took the light and went out, shading the light with her hand in order to see through the darkness.

She saw nothing in front of the door, nothing on the bench, nothing on the dung heap, where the old man used sometimes to sit in hot weather.

But, just as she was on the point of going in again, she chanced to raise her eyes toward the big apple tree, which sheltered the entrance to the farmyard, and suddenly she saw two feet—two feet at the height of her face belonging to a man who was hanging.

She uttered terrible cries:

"Victor! Victor! Victor!"

He ran out in his shirt. She could not utter another word, and turning aside her head so as not to see, she pointed toward the tree with her outstretched arm.

Not understanding what she meant, he took the candle in order to find out, and in the midst of the foliage lit up from below he saw old Amable hanging high up with a stable-halter round his neck.

A ladder was leaning against the trunk of the apple tree.

Victor ran to fetch a bill-hook, climbed up the tree and cut the halter. But the old man was already cold and his tongue protruded horribly with a frightful grimace.